Athie Wolfe

November 2010

Moondust

Autobiography of an Afterlife

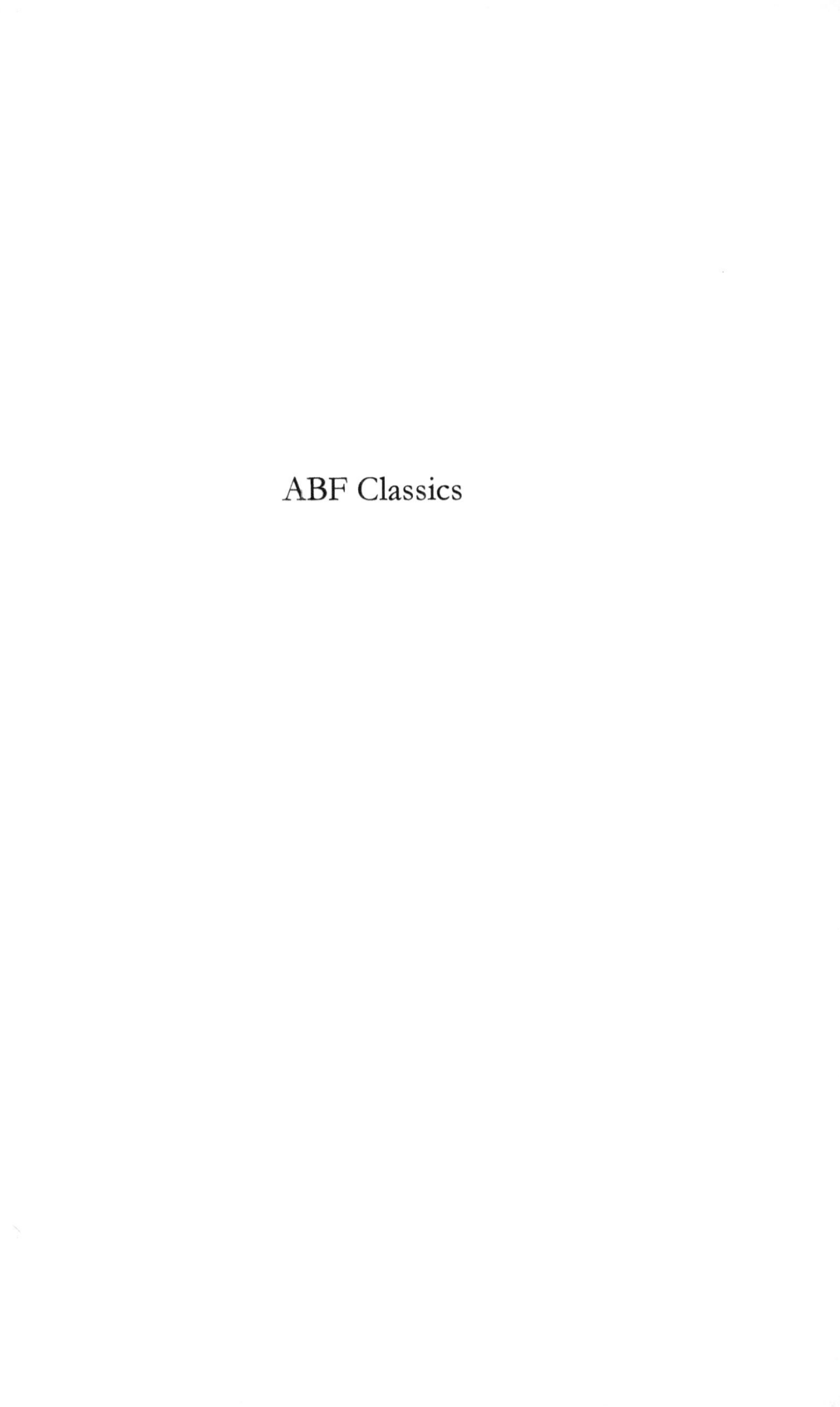

ABF Classics

Moondust stands out as an ode to our grandmothers and a witness to the possibilities and obstacles for progress across the generations. Feeling discouraged? *Moondust* inspires hope.

Yvonne Fenwick, *Psychotherapist,*
North Asheville, NC

A sweet and articulate portrayal of deep mystery and deep knowing—how these two truths have coexisted since the beginning. A triumph for Colleen and her word crafter, and a gift for the rest of us.

L. P. Spunkin, in *Catnap Journal*

This is not your typical ghost story, and that's due to the narrator's patience with her audience. Colleen won't resort to spooking you; instead, with utmost love and respect, she'll CHARM you into turning that page.

Betty Lou Laughter, *Natives of Burnsville*

If you read one book in 2011, pick this one. The planet, and your daughters, will thank you endlessly.

Amy Hanaford, *Artist, Monticello, MN*

Moondust is a good book. You'll be re-reading it three times before you pass it along, and after that, Colleen's words will linger in your dreams.

Isolia Nickerson, *Ph.D. Hermitology*

I'm in love with Colleen Nicholson; now I can't wait to meet her cousin Samantha McBroom in Athie Wolfe's next novel: *Sunbeam's Salamander* (due out June 2011).

Ben Livingston, MD

I've been reading Athie Wolfe for decades. Here's why.

Grace Anders, *Neighbor*

How many more miracles are out there? After reading *Moondust*, I suspect the answer is: uncountable. I'm eternally grateful for this timeless, encouraging story. A must-read for the 21st century.

Tripp Good, *Philanthropist and Skeptic*

A first-person account of the restlessness of womankind in the modern era, lovingly crafted. A treat for the mind and the heart.

"Doc" O'Barker, Author, *No Spin Guide to Meditation for Conservatives*

Just the thing for a cold winter evening and a cup of tea. With a biscuit, of course.

Annie Caneen, *Manicurist*

MOONDUST

Athie Wolfe

Athena Books of Fairview
January 2011

ABF

Athena Books of Fairview, NC

Copyright 2010

ISBN 978-0-9835346-2-4

Fairview, North Carolina

USA

Printed in the United States of America.

For Mother

A Matrilineal Genealogy

- **Colleen** Nicholson born 1881 died 1951

- Colleen's daughter **Emily** Nicholson Hanaford
  born 1896 died 1923

- Colleen's granddaughter Amy Ellen "**Elizabeth**"
  Hanaford Potter born 1920 died 2010

- Colleen's great-granddaughter **Cynthia** Elizabeth Potter
  and great-grandson Edward "**Ted**" Potter
  (Cynthia's Younger Twin) born 1949

- Colleen's great-great-granddaughter
  Della Potter Small born 1977

- Colleen's great-great-great-granddaughter
  Kierra Small born 2008

DEFINITIONS

EAVESDROPPERS.. .. Spiders, simply put. Spiders are known for dropping down from the rafters to listen in on your conversation, while you enjoy your tea on a Sunday afternoon. Occasionally they may land on your tablecloth or tea saucer, or even your head.

MOTHER LOVERS….. What we once called "witches." In recent times we have grown to understand that this was not a proper name but rather a terribly unfortunate epithet that intentionally promoted misunderstanding, fear and hatred of gifted, courageous women. Colleen says: "Even in your modern day, folks will flinch over the word 'witch,' and that is because the word has been chewed up and spit out so many times that it stinks anymore." Colleen refuses to use the word "witch," so you will find instead the name "Mother Lover" throughout her story.

RIVER OTTER….. In animal speak, Otter represents the feminine energy of life, containing elements of both earth and water. She helps us to see our own female nature, which is beautiful, nurturing, playful, and joyful. She expresses our solid connection with the river of life itself.

BLAME….. What Mother Lovers learned to do to themselves after the burnings, in order to protect themselves and their daughters from further mortal threat. In this clever way, they went into hiding but remained alive —they were allowed to live and give birth.

Colleen didn't know she herself carried this blame until she met baby Kierra. The current generation of Mother Lovers is shedding that blame like a crusty, dead skin —while spirits like Colleen and millions of grandmas cheer in the stands.

ONE

I've been watching them steady for a year, ever since they built their dream house twenty yards below my rock, scaring up not just ME but all the other elementals and untamed animals and eavesdroppers (mostly spiders) that inhabit my hillside. They're still too noisy for my comfort. I hear them talking (and arguing) late into the night while their baby sleeps. His voice is always loud, hers is hushed. They don't know it—or they choose not to know it—but their girl can hear them in her sleep, just as I can hear them in my current, stylishly slender ghostly form, which some would consider a type of sleep. But for the moment I'm awake, you understand, even if you think I am not really here.

I've been dormant, yes, for almost three decades, and I was coming to enjoy that "sleep," debating whether to ever awaken, when their construction—the banging and drilling and loud radio music, the occasional cussing that popped into the air like gun shots—all that unnecessary sound—stirred me up so bad I couldn't go back, especially after I saw who it was building the house: Della Small, one of my own! She's the spitting image of me. Watching her plant her garden last spring, that clinched it—the nasturtiums were the tipoff— she had to be my great-great-granddaughter, the one I glimpsed when she was first born, before this last long nap I've been taking.

Della's thirty-three years old, but she's only got one child. It's not for lack of trying; she's been with Tommy forever (from her perspective, not mine). They were high school sweethearts, engaged at age 20, and now she and Tommy are married twelve years. Eight of those years Della pursued parenthood with a vengeance, dragging Tommy with her. He complied after he learned his insurance would cover it, and finally Kierra was conceived in a doctor's office under bright fluorescent lights. Then Della almost miscarried at 18 weeks. She spent the final month of the pregnancy in bed. You might say Kierra came into this world with her ears back, reluctant for some reason only she knows, and to be sure her mama Della holds onto her like she's the last doll in the storefront window, the store she walked by day after day as a fatherless girl, hoping no one else would get that baby doll before she could save up the money and have her for herself.

They woke me for good with that blast of dynamite into a beautiful ten-ton chunk of granite that was getting in "their" way (how arrogant is that), and when I blinked and saw it was Della standing back there in the distance, her hands over her ears, all grown up, I vowed to stay awake for her lifetime if I have to, and then when I saw her little girl with the turned-in eye, the slanty eyelid.... oh my. Maybe there's a reason Della came knocking on my door. Pounding on it, rather. Breaking it down.

As far as I know, nobody remembers anymore what happened to me back in 1884, I think that's the year, but I've begun to grow rusty on my dates. I don't blame my people for their forgetfulness. That's the way it goes—we are allowed to forget the sufferings of our ancestors, or how could we ever get on with life? It's all too tragic, too poignant, isn't it? But since YOU are listening, and you do seem interested, I'll tell you how I got to being a ghost and all. Like most tragedies, my abandonment came with its own peculiar gifts. I was orphaned at the age of three—that was the tragedy for me, or so I thought—and that's also how I got my ability to see beyond time, I'm sure of it now, and that's why I am still here looking around, seeing into things most people don't get to witness even when their physical life is done, because they're in such a hurry to go directly up to heaven, I suppose. For me, I had something keeping me here.

Great loss gave me great vision. But I didn't make that connection, I certainly didn't want my fate, and by the time that knowledge caught me I was dead and that's the truth in black and white. That is to say, I didn't know what I was until I wasn't.

◯

During my days on this earth I remained a stubborn one. I died alone, the way I wanted it, completely alone in the woods, if "alone" means without humans. I walked up the side of the hill to the flat spot that overlooks the French Broad, my favorite place. Just beside the overlook, there was a naturally-occurring circle of hemlocks I named *Mother* when I was a teenager on the cusp of being married off. (I planned to be married there, the trees a stand-in for my mother.) The moon was only half full when I named those trees, and my man—Thomas—he died two days before the wedding. I was already pregnant with my only child. A girl, she grew up to be a tomboy like me, walking fence rails, throwing rocks, throwing off her shoes, climbing cliffs on Saturdays. That was it for me, in terms of marriage and children. I'm the original single mom.

Now I'm a single great-great-granny ghost, peeking through Della's window, soaking up the moonlight. There were a lot of bats tonight; I waited for them to finish their business with dinner before moseying over, because I do not like bats in my hair.

Della's walking her baby tonight. It's a little after 1am, and Kierra's fussing again, the little devil. She's had a run of colds and such, just little things. I heard Della tell Tommy it was because of the new "daycare." (What a funny word that is.) Fever, runny nose, cough, that sort of thing, old as the hills. Della says she might have to quit her job. She wrote in her journal that she wants to quit, but Tommy hates the idea. She wrote that, too (that he won't let her), then scribbled it out.

I'm not so keen on Tommy. He's a taker, that man. Really he's more like a boy than a man, always thinking about what he wants, planning, plotting. It's a wonder he ever agreed to have that baby in the first place. They fight nowadays more than they did when that house first went up, when I first poked my head around the corner to see who was there. The more they fight, the more she seems to get used to it, but I can see her mind bending, bending, bending in the unceasing hurricane winds of unhappiness.

She's walking her little Kierra, and that girl keeps pulling on her own little leg, like it hurts or something, and Tommy's snoring in the other room. I went in there and blew cold air across his face and mouth, to wake him up, but nothing. So I jumped on his stomach, and that did nothing but give him the hiccups. The hiccups didn't even wake him up—he's hiccupping in his sleep like a big baby, his stomach fat jiggling each time and I just feel cross. It's not that I'm sleepy, or hungry. Like I said, after three decades of snoozing I am wide awake, and you know I don't eat.

"There, there, there," Della's singing now. "Little mumpkin pumpkin, treasure of mine, getting too sleepy to stay up and whine."

I like Della's profile, that little white turned up nose, just like mine, the wispy curls. She looks about 15 years old. Her hair is thin, but shiny. She smiles like a milk saucer if you have any idea what I mean. That's how my mother described my own smile, a milk saucer smile, and she's got the green eyes to complement that smile, all twinkly and alive. Unlike me, Della would do anything for anyone, and she is beautiful to boot. She's getting too skinny though—I've noticed that too, in the past year. As if keeping her weight "under control" would solve everything, she just loses a pound or two every time she questions the marriage or her job or herself. This is unfortunate because she doesn't think as clearly when she starves herself. I don't like to think that she might not want to think. Ha!

Tommy moves his arms like he's having a bad dream; maybe it's a delayed response to my blowing on his face, or the end of those hiccups. Next thing we know he's up, he's peeing in the bathroom. He looks over into the next room, the baby's room, and he sees what's going on. "Honey, you okay in there?" he asks, and Della nods, "mmmm… hmmmm."

"You don't need any help?" he asks, but the answer is in his question and Della always says "no, go back to sleep honey," and the baby never wants her daddy anyway, he's loud and scary. Little Kierra already knows who cares about her, and of course she's already smitten with the one who doesn't take care of her—but not smitten enough to go to him for anything she needs.

I understand. It's pointless to wake up this husband.

Makes me so mad I could stomp on his stomach—no, that doesn't work… I could throw a lamp on him—just to interrupt his precious sleep, but all he would feel is the spider web feeling that maybe a bedbug has gotten on him, or the sheets came off and there's a breeze in the room. Della would notice the lamp lying there on top of him and freak out, and she has enough on her mind. Can you imagine what that's like for me? Can you imagine my frustration? Do you wonder why I stick around, when there's nothing I can do about it? Okay, maybe it is not much different from my actual earthly life as a female in the later part of the 19th century, we were pretty invisible then, too, but everyone had their place and there was some respect for our contribution, a mother was allowed to be a mother without having to be everything else too. I wasn't expected to be a sex object on top of being a mother. Whether the men respected us or not, men were willing to say out loud that they needed us and they lived up to our need for them—if they didn't die. It wasn't a sin to need each other back then. Women could live together whether or not they were lesbians and not much was said about it, at least, not where I lived out my life in the mountains of Western North Carolina.

That little thing, my sweet baby Kierra, she just keeps holding her leg and whining, and Della just keeps walking, back and forth, back and forth, back and forth. Their eyes are swollen, both momma's and baby's, one from lack of sleep, one from crying. Della presses her finger against Kierra's lymph nodes, feeling the swelling, evaluating.

Since I never sleep, I'll admit I appreciate the company, as selfish as that may sound to you.

For the most part, when I'm not angry and wanting to stomp something, I'm content with my new form. I am lighter than a feather, you know. I died just lying there on the ground, nothing dramatic. My last earthly vision? That same half moon that I saw when I named those trees as a teenager in love, a moon that is milk-white, pockmarked, imperfect to this day. That one thing remains unchanged since I died—I look up into the sky and I always see those hemlock fingers brushing about above me, as if to sweep away the dark sky so that I can see the half moon. Time stopped up there. Down below, time went on.

And maybe time becomes timeless when you die, but still there is an accounting of sorts. I started out dense, seen by many as I made my rounds. My unique face, my willowy nightgown, my old leather boots—there were testimonials about the old lady of Flat Top Mountain, and that was me all right. But as the decades wore on I did change, as I say, there was an accounting of sorts. I became thinner, more spread out, less... tangible. So yes, I'm timeless in one realm, but I do seem to respond to the time in your realm. I am, perhaps, wearing out.

Maybe if it had been a full moon I would have made my way onward to heaven, I could have been pulled right through that bright perfect circle into the wonderfulness, that place where there are no worries. But the half moon—I couldn't get my head through it. Even though my body had shrunk to eighty pounds, my skull remained round and hard and stubborn as ever. I knew it was time to let go of my body, but I also knew I wasn't finished raising my own girl, my one girl, my one chance. I knew something was unfinished, that I wasn't done here, and stubborn me, I wasn't going to allow one little thing like the loss of my physical body stop me from finishing my work. To this day I'm left gusting through these woods because of my own stubbornness and the pure hard-headedness of those girls that have come after me. They take after me. I pound on their heads to get through to them, but they don't listen. They can't see me, they won't see me. With all the freedom I have as a spirit, free of life and death, free to come and go, I still feel the way I felt under that rock when those people walked away without looking back. Helpless. Orphan. It's such a familiar feeling now, such a pain and yet a comfort. When I got free of my physical body, I went back to that rock first thing. It's who I am. I like to rest there. Sometimes I give up, and sometimes—like now—I give it all I've got.

The night that I died the half moon was turned upward like a cup, which foretells rain, and indeed it rained as soon as I was gone. It rained for three weeks straight, a hard, steady rain. The first sighting of me came after that, as the fog gathered its skirts and tiptoed out of the woods, and things began to dry, to look upward at the sun, and grow. A young boy found my body, it was Leroy Wilson's son, and that evening his mother saw my spirit walking through their apple orchard when she was putting the cows in. Back then, that first night, my spirit was so dense she thought I was a real physical person, she thought it was me, alive, and she called out to me but I kept going. An hour later her son came clashing into the kitchen with the news of my bones. I wish I could explain more on the subject of death than this, but ultimately, it's a mystery to me—I haven't crossed all the way over, and just like you, I can't

really conceive of it, that "final" place, I can't comprehend something like that with what's left of my mind, my ghostly mind. It's
just too big, we all might understand that. It's too big.

TWO

B ut there is one thing on my mind, still on my mind, a mission I keep up my sleeve, next to my heart, a mission I will not let go of until it is complete. I have a message for my female descendents. My hope now is to get through to my great-great-granddaughter Della, so she can pass it to Kierra, her little one with the crooked eye and the slanty eyelid. But I'm thinner, wispier than ever, and not only that, it's getting harder for them to listen. Kids these days. I know every generation says that, and believe me I have heard every generation say it, literally.

But in this 21st century it's harder than ever to get their attention. Kids these days! Yes I said "kids" even though my Della is more than thirty, because in so many ways it applies. They tune into television and computer and phone and they learn to drive when they are twelve. They move too fast, in too many worlds all at the same time, they don't see where they are, or where they are going, and I can't stop them for even a minute. By the time they reach their twenties, they want to be the kids they weren't, and that takes them up into their thirties.

I hate to say it, but the only way to make them listen is to LET them get hurt (not too difficult). This is hard to say. I'm tongue-tied. How do you let your loved ones get hurt? Easy. All parents do it even with the best of intentions. But I'm talking about, not just "give 'em a shove," or pinch their elbows—I mean the kind of hurt that tears away their very protection so that their outer skin—some of you are aware of it, that invisible cloak you all wear about six inches around yourselves day in and day out (it's what's left of me). With a sufficient scare, or trauma—whatever you want to call it these days—that outer skin rips. It makes a space for communication, it makes them open their ears, because sometimes, for some of them, if they get hurt enough they'll be left with a spiritual tattoo of sorts— they open up their ears and eyes to another realm. How can I describe it? It's like a bullet hole in a deer hide that you try to conceal. Some people can see it, some can't. Some people who mean to do harm are real good at seeing it, and they'll use it for harm. Some people who might as well be angels can see it too, and love you all the more for it. I can talk through that place, sometimes. I can see through it, whistle through it, make myself heard, and it's all for good. But mostly it's the animals that listen to me. Humans are another matter, and it's right to call them "humans" as distinct from "animals" because of this very problem.

Sometimes they hear me (my offspring) and I feel myself floating upward, released, my mission coming to fruition. Then they forget, and that's like an anchor pulling me back, they've gone back to that orphan state where they don't see themselves or take care of themselves and bad things happen. They can't pull me all the way down into their murky soup, but I feel the tug, the entrapment, the need. They listen, but only halfway. They see me, then they don't. Now we're well beyond the fourth generation of daughters, and again there is only the one girl. Her name is Della Colleen, her middle name is in my honor.

Della! Look at me! Set that down and look at me! (See! She glances at the ceiling, that's all I get.) Della, all grown up with a baby of her own. What year is it anyway? 2010?

Yes, 2010. Once an orphan, always an orphan. You television addicts like to think everything has a happy ending, even the commercials, and while that's true in my world it is not quite so concrete as you think it is, in your earthly world. An orphan doesn't know the physical feeling of a mother's love surrounding her child-body like a halo. I try to imagine how that would be, an earthly mother protecting my abundant child-soul, loving me with her very life, until well after I've gone on without her. Orphans give birth to orphans, did you know that? Just because they left me under that rock, three, four, five generations of daughters get to wear it. That's what bothers me. At heart I am a Mother Bear, and I want all my girls to know love, the love we orphan mothers missed. I'm impatient—the fabled seven generations is too long for me to wait. From this point of view I can see what they are missing and it is a lot, a lot.

Details. I know, Della will want the details, being young still. When humans reach a certain age, we have to be concrete before we can go anywhere else, I have learned that much in the past hundred years. Yes, symbolism and the afterlife work for two-year-olds, and in fact those things work for most children up until about the age of five, and sometimes, some people can hear that stuff again late in life after they've raised their children and their grandchildren. But there is a huge desert in the interim, where you just have to feed, feed, feed. Water, water, water. The nourishment HAS to be concrete, literal, full of words and sentences and food and sleep and exercise and activity and meaning. Having a human body is a lot of upkeep. Meaning, being human is the worst trouble maker of all, for this universe, I am telling you.

OK. Details, Della. No, I was not an orphan from day one. There was a time, now remembered only in my shoulders and in my heart, when a mother held me tight to her breast. There she is, bending over me, her body loving me, her arms holding me as if she could never let go, as if there were two of me, I am so abundant in her arms. Her blue eyes are caught on something else—some fear or danger on a horizon she's only heard about. Those were hard days, when babies died easily and parents lived into their fifties, if lucky. My mother had pale skin, reddish-brown hair, small blue eyes and strong hands. She was young—no more than twenty—on some big adventure to claim land with her husband and his brother, a sister-in-law, a cousin, and a half-dozen nieces and nephews. Wherever we went, there were always babies around. As far as I know, I was my mother's first living girl, the other two having died at birth. So—rather like Della—my mother clutches me like I'm her last chance, and at the same time she looks away from me, in case I die and leave her more bereft than she can bear. She thinks, as young people do, that there is a limit to what she can bear.

O

And my mother, she looks into the future as if she could know it, as if she could force the sun to rise tomorrow. Her eyes are harsh and longing at once. Her heart beats strong against my tiny velvet ear. I look up to catch her loving me, but she's always looking at something, or someone, else. Always, always, almost always, looking at something else, so why do I remember her eyes so clearly? Just an infant, I learn to look away too, but I have no idea what I'm looking for. I gaze at the sky, mistaking clouds for angels. What's Momma looking for? It must be important, and it's in the future because nothing important seems to be happening now. We are just living, after all, just eating and sleeping and living. Isn't that what we're doing?

What was I looking for, as a baby, staring up into the sky? Now, Della, I think it is you I was searching out all along. I've come to believe that. I watched you toddle around, watched you trying to make sense of the world while you went back and forth between your mother's house and your father's house. After a while it was too much for me, I fell asleep, lost you for a while, until now. Until you woke me up. Here you are all grown up, a child of your own to raise.

Listen to me, Della!

○

I really like the way I died. Don't pity that. I'd done all I could do with my physical body, and my mind was already starting to leave my body—I could feel it slipping away a little more, a little more each day, like some people lose their vision late in life. I'd been a hermit for about ten years, mostly because I just couldn't remember the things people want you to remember, which made conversation difficult and, frankly, no fun at all, especially when you factor in the truth that I never got on that well with people in the first place. So I did what I liked, what I wanted, to do. After Elizabeth left I wandered the tobacco fields with my last dog Elmore, in silence, then came home to drink my tea while Elmore slept under the table, his head on my feet. Looking at it from a 21st century point of view, I was most surely "dyslexic" in my living days. I think that is the word I heard Della use. I could not concentrate on book learning. I had a different way of thinking, and I was always a little off-balance. My right foot was smaller than my left, so when I ran I looked lopsided, like an otter caught on dry land. A river otter would understand me, and to be honest that's what felt like home to me most of my earthly life—water, and the world of animals.

Most people don't relate to that kind of a lifestyle, or don't admit that they might want it. You'll be shunned if you're too much of a loner. Ha!

Eventually, towards the end, I came to admit that—other than my granddaughter—I preferred my dog for company. When Elmore went on, when his grey nose twitched for the last time somewhere in the middle of spring, or was it the verge of spring—well, whenever it was, that was enough for me. No more people, and no more dogs. World War II had ended—as if there was anything I could do about that—and Elizabeth gone six years to parts unknown. It seemed like a good time to go, with no one left to take care of. Ha! Sometimes I do engage in wishful thinking, just like you do.

Besides, I was ready, past ready. So I spent several weeks—most of the summer, actually—eating a little less each day, until I was down to just some pure well water in the mornings. Then I walked away from the cabin Popo built (and died in), walked slowly up the slant to my old hemlock place. Those vibrant trees greeted me, knowing, not judging a thing, but knowing, and thanking me in advance for giving them my bones, I'm sure of it to this day. I watched—my body fed those trees for several years, after the Wilsons hiked up and buried me right where I lay, out of the kindness and understanding of their hearts. They knew where I wanted to be, I'm grateful it was Leroy found me. But those trees, my mother hemlocks, if they had tummies that could grumble their gratitude I would have heard it.

Feed your mother! She likes to eat!

To me, my private funeral was all about those hemlocks. It was perfect. They gave me a fine welcome and a fine goodbye. With the heel of my shoe, I dug a little place down into the pine bed where I could sink in and feel surrounded by my mother trees. It was as if they were embracing me, cradling my spirit even before I got down into my little earthly crevice. I faced the sky. Autumn leaves of gold and red swirled down around me, sometimes landing on my face. The temperature ... perfect. After a couple days—it didn't take long—I floated out of my body and got caught, like traces of spider web, in the lacy hemlock branches. Those hemlocks served as my only witness, those trees being the only mother I ever trusted, their arms intertwined as if to create one body, one tree, one mother. Who gets to die with their mother in attendance? Not many. My last vision was a river otter, I swear, she looked to be the same one that trotted out from beneath that rock the day they left me there, another mother of sorts, a creature that would smile at you, one that aims to live, and play, without apology. So you see, there can be a happy ending, but it is not the happy ending you want to imagine. I died happy; don't think I'm lingering because I died alone. I died the way I wanted to die.

In fact, I liked dying better than being born, better even than being young. It was less violent, and less lonely, and somehow, more young.

But I know, I know, death is not of great interest to you Della, not now when you need to focus on the living. You want details. My name? Colleen. Date of birth? Somewhere around the late 1870's or early 1880's. I never saw a birth certificate, but years later (when I'd become a grandmother) a Western doctor did mark it on a piece of paper after looking at my teeth and skin. My girl Emily—your great-grandma—made me go to the doctor right after she gave birth to Amy Ellen Elizabeth in the hospital, Emily being the first of your ancestors to give birth in a hospital. And she got flat-out mesmerized by Western Medicine at that point in time. Emily insisted I should go to the "real" doctor, so I went, to please her. Nothing to come of it.

It cost twenty-five dollars and fifty cents to have her baby in a hospital and a man helping instead of a woman. My Emily rejected the Mother Lovers, you see.

○

As for me, I came into the world someplace out east, Massachusetts, probably, in some back bedroom. There's an old family grocery store we were connected with back there, still in business to this day, but the name's changed a few times so I heard. It's no longer called Nicholson's, I know that much.

My first year of life was lived in Western Civilization, known simply as "civilization" back then. In my second year, seeing that I stayed alive long enough to learn how to walk, they decided it was safe to take a chance and travel south, then west. Actually, it was probably my father who decided that, since he took my mother away from all the support she had—that being her maiden aunt Lucille and several female cousins. They'd never had money, of course—we don't come from that—but out east they had each other.

My mother and her new sister-in-law, Beatrice, barely knew each other when the small clan headed off to explore and perhaps claim some wilderness, while wilderness still existed. My father's brother had gone up to Maine for a couple of months and brought Beatrice home with him the week before they all started out on that journey, and she was young to boot. Mother and Aunt Beatrice disliked each other from the start, Mother being quiet and self-contained, accustomed to fending for herself, while her sister-in-law cried for help every time she stubbed her toe no matter how often it happened. Beatrice was superstitious, and mean for her age. They got as far as the Blue Ridge Mountains when Beatrice discovered she was pregnant and the little group decided to pull over for a year or so, camping right there in the mountains.

Then it goes blank. I don't know what happened, or why, them hiking single file to get out of that place, hiking for days, getting lost, Beatrice's baby brand new to this world but something wrong with it—it didn't cry, it hardly even wiggled. I think it was a boy, but I have lost any images for that baby, just like I lost most of the sense of my own mother and father. There was some urgency, some danger, whether it was the native peoples or post-Civil War bullies or some kind of animal threat, I don't know.

And then, suddenly, I was under that rock, alone, and them hiking away from me like water pouring out of the tea kettle, they were gone, draining my soul out from my body, taking my very blood with them. I'm reaching up to the sky, howling with all my will to live, and the reply from the sky and the rock and the footsteps and the dirt? Silence. It is too poignant. You probably can't stand even hearing me tell it, all these years later, the silence of it, the deadly silence, providing no comfort for a dying child.

THREE

No, wait, there is one sound: water. Loud water, a creek rushing past me, humming, talking to itself, spitting on me every so often with cold crystal-clear droplets across my forehead, perhaps well-intended but no comfort in it, no comfort at all. I am alone, hungry, thirsty, losing weight by the minute. I am losing myself and the only way I can describe it is that there were two of me, and now there is only one of me, walking away. I am three years old, old enough to walk, to run, yet I can't move—I must be very sick. I'm lying on my back when I lose all consciousness, and off I drift up into the sky, my little cobweb soul. I watch my spirit walk away down the same path as those other people, running as if to catch up with them, then I turn my head away.

I'm sorry Della, I don't know why they left me there. I don't know if they planned to come back for me. To be honest, I don't even know who left me there, though I assume it was my parents, but maybe they were killed off, and someone else had me? Whoever they were, I don't know where they went. That part is gone for good. I can tell you everything that's happened since then, but the past is blank, dead; the light's gone off for good and I can't see a thing back there in that empty old closet. It makes me cough, all the dust in there.

My next memory—after a long spell of drifting skyward and swimming through the sky forever, for who knows how long—my next memory is the awkward scratchy touch of an adult man's hands, a pale man with light brown hair, streaks of white just in the back, some kind of overalls and a cotton shirt, leather coat. He's picking my body up out of the dust, putting a hand on my forehead, setting his cheek against my little chest. His name, I will come to learn, is Sandy Castleman, and he has a dog with him, a white dog,

with pointy feathery ears, named Runner. Sandy's a bachelor far-
mer, eking some small portion of life out of the slanty, rocky soil up
above this creek. He lives alone, I'll come to learn, because he
doesn't fit in with the town people, but not because he's mean.
He's Jewish, but he keeps that under wraps—I didn't even know it,
and me his adopted daughter, until after I myself had died and cir-
cled back to visit the town, and read it in the papers my granddaughter inherited (I couldn't read when I was still alive, but since
then I've had plenty of time to learn it).

He's not mean, Sandy, there's nothing wrong with him. Actually, he's kind enough to take me in when most practical folks
would have kept on walking—back in those days, a baby was a li-
ability, especially a girl baby, and sick at that. Well, he's got me in
his arms, my head hanging down. I'm completely unresponsive.
He's got to do something with me, because that's how Sandy
thinks, he feels responsible more so than most. He carried me into
town directly that first day he found me, even though it was getting
on into the afternoon, but after Sandy described my symptoms the
town doctor refused to treat me, to keep me overnight, refused
even to see me beyond one hasty glance under the blanket Sandy
wrapped me in. Whatever I had, I was doomed. Then Sandy took
me up higher onto a ridge above his cabin where some native peoples were camping under the stars, people he knew would not fear
my crossed eye. One of the women up there gave me something
bitter to drink. She took me out of Sandy's arms and forced me to
drink it, then she held me for a long time before releasing me back
to Sandy, instructing him that he was supposed to be my mother
now, and my father as well, and I could smell the spirits on her
breath, and feel Sandy nodding as one hypnotized. Somehow he
understood the idea behind her words and although he agreed to do
it, Runner's the one who really mothered me the most in those early
years. Men don't have a lot of that kind of instinct in them; some
dogs have more than most men. That was true of Runner, being a
female dog. She was a good mother, and a good doctor, in retro-
spect. Lucky for me, really—doctors back then had a reputation for
killing you, not on purpose, but still.

○

Lucky for me also, that Runner was even younger than me, she hadn't quite completed her first year of life and I was already three, or thereabouts, when I got transplanted into that family—Sandy for a father, Runner for a mother. Because I was three and she was one, Runner stood by me for the following fourteen years, slept beside me, ran beside me, followed me to school the one full year I attended, waiting for me outside the schoolhouse under the sourwood by the southern path. After that we got into a habit of walking through the woods when the moon was full, that's how Sandy came to calling me "Moondust," but only on those bright moon nights when we came in late, otherwise I was just Colleen, plain old Colleen Nicholson. Runner did not teach me to comb my hair, to put it up in a bun, to bathe every day, nor to pinch my cheeks to make them red or bite my lips and lick them to make them shiny. Runner could not tell me I was pretty or sew me a dress. But Runner was better than that; she stood with me, she looked me in the eye like no human ever did, not even my man Thomas on the day your great-grandma Emily was conceived. I believe Runner lived to fifteen years old on my account, because she was a large thing, not the kind of dog that should make it that long, especially in those days before veterinarians became part of the family like in your case, Della, when you had that little white and yellow dog that you got for Kierra when she was just a baby. A dog and a baby at the same time—that was a little too much especially when you factor in those modern vet bills. Back in my day nobody had insurance for the doctor, we used money or chickens. The idea of insurance for a dog? As my Della likes to say, I won't even go there.

....And somewhere during those years of my growing up, Sandy Castleman married a native woman from that high ridge, a relative of the Mother Lover who healed me. About two years before I had my baby, they had theirs. But that woman couldn't teach me how to be a white woman, either. What she could teach was herbs, all kinds of herbs.

○

Della, you're my last hope, not the last hope, but MY last hope, because there just isn't much left of me now. I can feel that certainty like you can feel the beach sand under your feet, I've heard you tell of it even if I haven't ever touched sand myself, with my feet or otherwise. I am trudging towards it, my time. The lighter I get, the quicker I go. I can almost make out the white, haloed form of Runner on the path up ahead of me. That Runner, she was faster than some horses. I'll never catch up.

Della's the spitting image of me, doesn't have a clue about that—why would she? For all I know, she IS me, recycled. She's getting out of bed now, before noontime, on a Saturday, because she has work. She's having a flashback in time, to her first restaurant job, and I'm watching the flashback with her: It's her first job, a hostess for Shoney's, and I'm proud to say she's good. She shows up on time, she's friendly and fast about her work, and she gets her homework done too. She's what they still call a "good" girl, even with all the feminism and women's rights and the vote and all that, and there's nothing wrong with being good, it's just the way THEY mean it.

She's a "good" girl all right. I mean "Good" with the capital "G" and nothing in it for people who want to use her up. Tommy says he loves her, then he undercuts. I see it bright and clear as the noonday sun, and just like the sun, Tommy gets in my eyes, especially when he says he loves her. I just don't see it. When he tells her he loves her it's just words, words that confuse her mind, bend her vision of her own life. By now she's about to break. She's as vulnerable as I was, being an orphan like me, in a way, her mother Cynthia at work sixty hours a week since Della was three months old. That man never married Cynthia, but he stuck around for a while, just long enough to get Della all mixed up, going back and forth from house to house. That's crazy! We are not making progress on this mother thing. My descendents have more stuff, and they spend more time at work, they have the vote, but those are the only differences, we are still orphans. I've been watching this go on for generations, and it's true, the circumstances might change, might change a lot, but people hang onto the same old feelings, hang on like a dog hangs onto an old bone, and my own people are no exception to that. I'm telling you, it is very frustrating from my point of view.

As long ago as the Salem Mother Lover burnings, my people—the females, that is—have aspired to be "nice" and being smart, we have pretty much succeeded. We are good at whatever we set our minds to. The attacks on Mother Lovers back there then, like a long deep cut, they left a deep impression. After that, a woman would want to be "nice" at all costs, knowing how big it counts. We would receive that compliment on a regular basis, that we are either "nice" or "sweet" or both. Being nice keeps us under control, I guess. It reassures the so-called Christian society. Society wants its SMART women to be NICE women. This means we don't express any anger about how things are, we don't complain when we feel used, or used up. We hide behind our own skirts, just as our Mother Loving ancestors learned to hide their treasure of knowledge beneath an accommodating smile. You can hide something for so long you forget where you hid it, and all the while it's right there where you left it. We scold our daughters for having a true imagination, and life goes on.

There's always someone less fortunate to think of, always the other person's point of view to consider, always somebody to please. Be nice, that's the way to be a woman in this world. That's how you ward off the self-named judges who can make your life miserable or even end it for you. Sometimes a smart woman can find a man who respects and treasures her; sometimes she finds a man who uses her, who uses her up. That's life, I suppose—a lot of dumb luck involved. But why not change that if you can? Are we supposed to just sit down on our luck, like a seat assignment?

So I know, you wonder why I'm so urgent about this. You don't see the problem. After all, our people are getting along well enough, loving, giving birth. Our line has survived. It's a maternal line, but not very powerful, and that is because I was an orphan. You think I'm a fussy old thing, a frustrated old ghost, stuck in my own past. You want to send a psychic to help me move along to the next world? If that's what you're thinking, you are wrong!

My dear baby Kierra—my lovely Della's daughter—she has a calling and nobody knows it yet. If Della gets sidetracked now we've had it—men, women, children… earth and spirits alike. We will cease to exist if there's no one left to remember me, YOUR MOTHER. No. I am not moving on. Not just yet. While I didn't mind giving up my physical body all those generations ago, I don't want to lose this cobwebby one that can still speak out. Besides. It's light and easy here and, to me, still very pretty. I can come and go, I can glisten like a rainbow in the sun, and I seem to last forever and ever, on and on. Quite a few of the animals can see me because they understand timelessness, and we do converse from time to time when things are slow in all dimensions.

Sometimes my mind—or whatever it is—works like this: I can be right here on Della's doorstep watching the first star appear (which takes forever if you keep your eye trained on the sky, nothing else to do). Then I am back in time more than seven decades, watching the afternoon sun bounce off George Apple's shiny black hair, him stretching his arm across the picnic table to hold my granddaughter Elizabeth's slender perfect hand. And I get goose bumps. Then I'm floating in the creek on a quiet afternoon, feeling it rush through me all icy, when suddenly I'm watching little Ted take his first swim in his grandpa's pond (he didn't jump in, he fell in). Or I'll be longing after the moon one minute, and the next thing I know I'm sitting beside Della in the back seat of her mama's car; she's glorying in her first Goo-Goo Cluster, holding it up high, looking at it with great greedy love before she eats the whole thing.

O

No doubt about it, Della's my new favorite person and she will remain so for a long time. She's got my shiny, wavy, reddish-brown hair, with pixie eyes and little fresh ears that stick out. Freckles scatter across her nose and cheeks and chin, and frankly she is adorable, but she has no idea about that. What I love about her is her heart, she's as giving as Christ himself, and just about that pure. She loves the world. Deep down in her heart she's loyal to her momma Cynthia (my great-granddaughter) 100 percent, even though she hardly saw her mother growing up, even though Cynthia gets on Della's nerves whenever they actually talk, and even though Cynthia has moved all the way to Seattle to be geographically close to her own mother, Della's grandma, Amy Ellen Elizabeth. (There's always something, or somebody, that needs taking care of.)

These days, Della can't sleep at night, because her little girl's been sick so much. She's got the shadowy grey circles under her little green eyes and that makes me sad. Sad, because I know where it leads, and because I know what needs to happen before another generation goes by, and because I am running out of ideas for contacting these people who act like they're deaf even though they are my own DNA and they should be listening to me, out of respect for their ancestors or the possibility of spirits, if nothing else. I am RIGHT HERE, Della. I do my best to talk like you, and still you don't hear me.

Long ago, Della asked Cynthia about me, but her mother couldn't answer her questions—she just didn't know, never having wondered much about such things herself. Cynthia's got too much on her plate to go researching the past. And Della's grandmother—Elizabeth, my Emily's girl—she can't remember anything that happened before the war because of two things—that run of shock therapy she went through, and the Alzheimer's. Please don't be depressed. This isn't one bit depressing, it's just life with its ups and downs. After the shock therapy, Amy Ellen Elizabeth lost some chunks of time, but she felt better, and she never got that depressed again, even now that she's losing the rest of her memory. Perched in the porch rafters of her nursing home, where I sometimes like to mingle and gossip with the eavesdroppers, I have heard her say on several occasions that if she was allowed to choose she'd rather stay in a good mood than get her memory back. She even said it when no one (except me) was listening. She sits in her rocking chair, half body, half spirit, her memories scattered like dandelion fluff, her heart outside her body. I suspect she's faking the Alzheimer's but the doctors are convinced.

Della, believe me, time is running fast through the neck of the sand bottle. Tommy wants to mooch off you—I know, I heard, he graduates in the spring, it's true, it's looking good on paper, he does go to both school and work—but he's getting all set to slack off, because you make the better money at that fancy restaurant, even if it is killing you, you're doing it and he sees that paycheck. And what have I seen? I, Coleen Nicholson, have seen him,

Tommy Small, on the computer doing that gambling stuff, losing your money. I would testify in court, honey. He sees that you are the hard worker, and a pretty face, and you let him manage the money, and that's enough for him. You give everything to him! He sees someone to baby him for the rest of his life, Della, you being so motherly to others, so guilty if THEY aren't happy.

Be motherly to yourself, Della! I know why you're not— you're not motherly to yourself because I was an orphan over a century ago. Yes, I take the responsibility. Not that it was my fault that I was an orphan, but it is a fact that I was an orphan, and you can pin your low self-worth on that event all the way back then. It's generational, rolling merrily down the slopes from one baby to the next to the next to the next, like no one can stop it, a runaway boulder with no wall to stop it, no valley to rest in, no plateau in sight. It's got to stop, or you will stop, and you will not live to raise your child. Listen to me.

I hope Della can hear me; she doesn't appear to be listening a whit. "Tommy, can you drop me at work tomorrow morning?" Della texts him. "Sry," he answers 20 minutes later, "I hv 2 work 2." But he doesn't, you see, he doesn't HAVE to work at all and he never cared about spelling either, even before texting. His employer gives him four hours on Monday and Wednesday nights, and this is Saturday night. He's got leeway even on the days he's scheduled. I found that out, floating over his place of employment where he makes those sales calls; I saw the schedule and I heard him talk his way out of an evening's work in order to play a game of cards with Uncle Ted and some other allies, over at Alvin's place. Sure, people do that when they're young, but Tommy's in his 30's and he has a child.

Another time he begged out of work and met some girl named Tiffany at the Waffle House. Well, he said something that offended Tiff and she took off in her rusty old Honda, but then I saw her car again at one of those gentlemen's clubs, parked not far from his. I just didn't want to go there, I felt something very dense and negative streaming out of the concrete blocks that formed those windowless walls, so I didn't go in, I curved around, did a U-turn back home, and after that I stopped tracking Tommy. No, I didn't see anything going on, nothing at all, not one thing. I just didn't like the smell of it. Maybe he was trying to help that girl; I'll never know.

FOUR

Uncle Ted wouldn't hang around a place like that. One thing I remember, watching Ted and his sister Cynthia as young ones just starting out in life, they both had the sweetness, what I call the Nicholson sweetness. It's a kind of natural compassion that you can't help, it's just in you. It's unusual for a man to have it as much as Uncle Ted does, but he does. I had a touch of it myself, even though I was half tomboy, and my mother had it so much that she couldn't eat meat, so I heard, it came down to me from Sandy Castleman and I don't know how he knew, I never thought to ask him. She was a vegetarian, but that was way back when, you understand, and it explained some of her sickliness I am sure. Speaking of sickliness, I know what happened to Ted, him only nineteen and drafted into Viet Nam (he insists on spelling it like that so I honor him by using the two words, not one).

With a heart like his, he couldn't last and he didn't, not on the inside. He went through the motions as instructed and came out the other end intact and on time and with no official dishonor, but something happened involving a child, he's blacked it out so that I can't see into it, he tore those pages out of the book. Something happened there in Viet Nam and he came back from that place a different person on the inside, as different as a person can be without splitting in two. At first, he kept up appearances as much as he could: There was that brief marriage to the cute, short little blond—Debbie—who fled him after two months, no kids. Then he worked a series of sales jobs, from auto dealerships to cemetery franchises, whatever he could find within 50 miles of home, sometimes living with friends, other times going back to the family cabin on Bear Mountain. Each new job would start out well enough. He'd make a good first impression, tell them whatever

they wanted to hear, and before a week or two had passed he'd
show up late. Then he'd miss a day. He'd get a warning. The next
day, he'd NO-SHOW, so's to SHOW them who's boss. He'd either get himself fired or quit before they could fire him. Word got
around and they stopped hiring him in this county, and he didn't
have the nerve to move anywhere else. It's like he was frozen, his
feet stuck in icy mud. He couldn't find a thing to do around here,
but he didn't seem to mind too much. He got used to it. He had
his weekly poker game, and he had a steady relationship to tend to:
his alcohol, the liquid hitch-hiker he picked up in Viet Nam, got
attached to, brought home with him to meet the family, and finally,
married. He fed it, tended it, grew it into something big until it was
the main thing about him. It's as if the alcohol liked being the center of his life.

In return, the whiskey gave him some pleasure, some relief,
and protected him from the questions. When they saw that he had
an alcohol problem, people backed off from asking what he did in
Viet Nam, or even what he's doing now, for that matter—who is he
dating, where does he work, what are his plans, his hopes. Alcohol
does away with those types of conversations; instead, any true
friends of his are much more invested in the task at hand—for example, trying to get the car keys from him, bailing him out of jail, or
not bailing him out, getting him to eat something. Pressing him to
get help. After a while, Ted's true friends dropped away and he was
left with the remnants, people like him, people getting along without a compass or a plan. Finally only Ted's sister was left to care
what happened to him; Cynthia shadowed him for ten years trying
to get him into a program, and failing that, trying to get him to eat
at least two meals a day, and failing that, she moved herself to Seattle to be closer to their mother, instructing her daughter Della not
to get involved with Uncle Ted. "He's not your problem," she said.
"He's got to hit bottom so don't get in his way, the faster he hits
bottom, the better off we'll all be."

For the most part Della's complied with that advice, though
she couldn't say no to the man if he showed up at her house. She
sees the sweetness in him under that mask of alcoholism and she
has the family compassion, the idea that he might recover even after
all these years. She thought her baby might inspire him, but as
Kierra grew from infancy into a toddler, and her skin tone unex-

plainably deepened to a warm nuggety brown and her hair curled up around her ears, Ted quit coming over. He practically hid from her. "Good," Cynthia said. "You don't need him around when you're trying to raise a baby. You've already got two babies." Cynthia should have said "three babies" because Della's a baby too. Aren't we all?

It's Saturday night. Della's lucky to have the Sunday brunch shift, it's very good tipping, but she needs a ride in. She stares at her phone, trying to make sense, surprised that Tommy has to work on a Sunday, but accepting that without thinking further because that's one of those things she would rather not think about. After all, it's really not surprising. Della knows that Tommy won't help, whatever his "reason." While it does not make sense, she IS used to it. Does that make sense? If it does, tell me about it.

"OK," she texts back. "I'll call Liz to come get me… my car's ready—I can get it in the afternoon. I'll give them a call."

"2morrows Sun," he texts back. "U cnt get car."

"The gate'll be open," she replies. "I'll call Liz."

"Try Ted," Tommy texts again. "He got hs car bk." Tommy must be feeling a little guilty, to bother to add this extra bit of advice, but Uncle Ted drives drunk and besides, she hasn't seen him in months and she wouldn't want to give him any ideas about coming over. She sets the phone down, combs out her dry, fluffy hair with rapid strokes. (I like her hands, so soft and young. I lived to be seventy, produced a daughter, died under the stars— but sometimes it all just seems like a long and fancy dream, in contrast to Della's strong young life, so concrete, so real.)

○

Sometimes it's as if there were two of me, one still under that rock, the other walking away, walking away, being dragged, in fact, away from me. Who stayed? Who left? I was three. Part of me remained under the rock? Forever? My life ended when I was three, my life as I knew it. That's what it means to be an orphan. It is death. When our little Kierra turns three next summer I plan to be there to see her celebrate. You can understand what it means to me. I plan to help her blow out the candles. I would not, could not, miss that. Kierra, my offspring, alive and well in the 21st century! This is the generation that will end the curse, I know it in my deepest heart. Kierra will not be orphaned, she will BLOSSOM at three, she will spill forward toward a life of great creativity, joy, energy! I see it, and we'll all go on from there, the beautiful Nicholson women, stretching out to create the future in every direction, a future for everyone.

What happened to my own little one, my Emily? Seems like she appeared, then disappeared, in a flash, a phantom, a dream, that girl. I hardly knew her. My tomboy sweetheart, you'd have thought she was a boy the first seven years of her life, trying to make up for Thomas being gone. She grew up all right, my sweet girl, grew up and lived long enough to have a girl of her own, Amy Ellen Elizabeth, who had herself a set of twin babies (Cynthia, and Cynthia's brother Ted). I looked in on all that, you see, and I even helped with some of the naming. I have the vantage point to do that. I come and I go, but I generally like to show up for the births and deaths—I have a front row seat, after all. Much of the middle part is boring. I can pick and choose.

Funny thing, there's a blank spot over some parts of my memory when it comes to my own girl. Sweet Emily. When she turned three, something went blank in me for a while, it's like I abandoned myself, couldn't see myself, couldn't see my girl. I can't explain it other than that. Nothing going on around me, a blank terrain, a blank horizon, radio silence. Except I do remember one thing. I remember Runner... she died when my Emily was, oh, around that age. Three. There I was, 18 years old, no husband, and a little girl to raise all by myself, working the garden and trading with Vic Holmes (we called him Mr. Vic), trading my carrots and potatoes for dry goods, feeding old Runner on garden scraps and stale bread, taking in sewing for the Christian ladies who wanted to help me but not that much. By the time Emily was three I was handling things pretty well, yes, I do know that. It looked like we'd make it even though the Christian town peoples didn't think much of us, me an orphan, raised by a Jew who married an Indian, my daughter and me with the same last name of Nicholson. At best, they pitied us. A woman of unknown religion struggling to raise a little baby girl is not a threat so long as you stay on the outskirts. They tolerated us all right, although above all else, my lack of a husband meant I was "less than." You know how that goes.

We were making it. Then Runner died—old age—and right after that, within the month, my main customer, Mr. Vic, shot himself by accident and we had to move down the road to find work, and my Emily refused to let me call her by her pet name, "Nicholson," ever again. It was as if she had a panic attack whenever I said it, so I stopped, as much as I loved our family name. To me it means sweetness, innocence, kindness. Hope.

Hmph. Strange, I hadn't thought of Runner in a hundred years, and here she is sitting in my mind's eye, extending her paw for a shake and a treat from Mr. Vic.

Runner liked the bones Mr. Vic brought. Emily liked the sweets. Vic Holmes was the last good help to us for many years, until I finally got in with the Hanaford family, ex-slaves from South Carolina who had a small farm, they needed an extra hand and so they took me and Emily in, because they needed us and because they were good folk. By then Emily was marrying age, and she took to Mrs. Hanaford's widower brother, Samuel, even though he was 20 years older and a grandfather himself. They had that baby girl Amy Ellen Elizabeth, a beauty, and then Emily herself died three years later from an infection that ran over her like a train. Yes, that happened. I don't like to tell it, but it happened. There's my little granddaughter but three years old, an orphan like me. That's the second time I left my body, that I know of anyway. I screamed that night, flew off, taking a dozen shingles off the roof as I went screeching, bending the trees back and forth like to break them, then when I'd done all the damage I could do, and still that little girl Elizabeth an orphan.

○

I could not bring her mother back. I nearly wanted to die, myself. But that came soon enough, and years later as a ghost I had to do some looking to find her, but there she was, a grown-up, handsome Amy Ellen Elizabeth Hanaford, passing for white in a little town in upstate New York, freshly married to a man by the name of Potter. She shortened her name to Elizabeth Potter, and that was that. I could have lost her, sleeping as long as I did. That man she married, I never knew his first name because everyone just called him Potter. He had the bluest eyes I've ever seen, and what he liked about Elizabeth was her dark brown eyes. He adored her. She told Potter and his people that she was an orphan, which was only half true. She never looked back, and she never felt at home in the north, either. She missed her old black grandma more than anyone else in the world, even more than me, and kept on missing her even after her twin babies came along, black-haired and blue-eyed, white and freckled and new.

O

Another long night. Long night after long night. Thank goodness, Kierra's finally sleeping. Della needs to get some rest so she can get up for work tomorrow. Tommy will make breakfast, that's one thing I'll give to him. He does it without being asked, and he doesn't burn things the way Della does. Liz can't, but Monica has agreed to give her a ride in the morning. Della walks as softly and silently as a monk with that precious sleeping lump of humanity heavy in her arms, passing the crib (which has yet to be used), easing her skinny hips down onto the bed. Della slowly flops down sideways so that she is half-lying on the bed now, still holding Kierra tight, trying to fool Kierra into thinking her mother is still walking her. This time, it works. A half an hour later, Tommy tiptoes in; moments after he hits the pillow, he's snoring, one heavy hand flopped across Della's belly. It doesn't even occur to her to wonder what he's doing here when he said he had to work in the morning. Or to ask where he was last night. She has other things on her mind. Kierra stays asleep for four hours, so long as Della lies right beside her and does not let go of her, until the alarm wakes them all at eight.

Sometimes I go to work with Della, sometimes I go along to the daycare with Kierra. Today I will go with Della and hang around the Five-Star restaurant where she LIVES forty-plus hours of the week. I'll watch over my Della today. Besides, I'd like to get a peek at Monica, Della's other girlfriend from work, who's giving her a ride today. Della is scheduled on days all this month, so she can drop Kierra off on the way, and pick her up at closing time. The daycare is in a church, which is a comfort to Della for some reason, the colorful messages on the walls about love and such.

The ratio is one "teacher" to six two-year-olds, which is pretty good in this town, and Kierra's in love with one of the assistants (Miss Tracy), which helps. On Sundays it's a little different; with church going on, there are two extra classes and more kids overall, but she can still drop Kierra there, which is a Godsend. Ha!

Today Della will again set her daughter into that noisy mess, wishing (I can read wishes, when they are strong) that she could set her baby into someone's arms rather than drop her onto her own little two-year-old feet in the middle of chaos, a vast playroom floor scattered with toys and confused-looking tots walking in tiny circles. Hurriedly, she'll find a huge plastic block and set it into Kierra's fat little hands, then hug her goodbye, fast and tight, and try to leave before Kierra cries. She doesn't always cry, of course. And sometimes, when Della comes to pick her up, she's not ready to go.

The babysitter they had before, Betty, I think was her name? Yes. She always held Kierra in a warm, firm hug each day as they waved goodbye to Della. But then Betty's old husband had to have a heart attack, and she had to give up the daycare during his recovery, which is going on six weeks now. Every morning, Della misses Betty. I do too.

Della moves quickly, running almost-late as usual. She's wearing her black Earth Shoes (which work best for a long day on her feet), with her black sleek slacks and the black v-neck with the three-quarter sleeves that's required for waitpersons. She'll don that gold glittery apron when she walks through the back door into the kitchen, and begin another day of pleasing others. Oh, she's good at that, my Della. Everybody likes her, or at least it is safe to say that everyone appreciates her. She smiles with her whole face. She does her job and then some. She's always scanning the tables for crumbs and empty salt cellars, a bouquet that's shedding its petals. She walks about with the sweeper and goes under the tables a second, third time. She helps her compatriots carry out orders for the larger tables. She smiles as if she cares, because you know what?— she cares. She wants people to feel loved, to feel happy, to know she sees them, and those are just her customers I am talking about. Where did she learn such love? From her mother? Somewhat, but I like to think it is in the genes, that Nicholson sweetness, and I will take some distant credit for that.

Monica's at the curb honking, and Della's sprinting out the door, beginning the daily marathon, Kierra on her hip. Monica swings by the church daycare and keeps the car running while Della dashes in, deposits Kierra in the middle of Room 3, fetches the block, sets it into her daughter's plump hands, and today, the blankie also, because Kierra feels poorly, too poorly to whimper as she watches her mother running out of the room, back to Monica, off to work. It gives me a flash of my old trauma, seeing that. I'm watching my own mother going down that path away from the rock and out of sight, me sick, my arms in the air. She didn't come back. You'd think that would be dead history by now, and it is, to Della, but to me? It still plagues me now and then when I least expect it. I don't mean to complain, it's not at all the grief it once was. I have so much to be grateful for now, my many generations of offspring, my ability to fly here and there, even materialize when I need to, from one location to another, in the blink of your eye. So I'll shake it off, and get on with the day, because that's my wish for Della also and I know she feels my presence. I've noticed, sometimes, she even picks up on my mood.

FIVE

S he's indeed got a day ahead of her, my dear Della. It's coming into tourist season and already the hotel next door is full. They stream in, breakfast, brunch, lunch, throughout the day, the usual mix, most of them polite and friendly since this is, after all, an expensive place to eat, and few people get rich without learning something about public manners. There are some cranks from time to time, but not as many as you would think, despite that idea that rich people are impossible to please and leave small tips. Della will do well today, she'll bring in $200+ in tips. She'll squirrel away $50 into the account that Tommy doesn't know about, and the rest will cover three full days of Kierra's daycare at the church. But I'm getting ahead of my story now; it's still morning, a fresh sun shining on Della and Monica as they hurry into the restaurant. Della looks worried, but I think it is only the sun in her eyes. Her thoughts are not coming through to me at all, as if she's deliberately concealing them, even from herself.

They walk, half-run across the parking lots to the employees' entrance, pocketbooks and keys jingling. Bam, they're inside, immersed in the hot noise of a busy kitchen. Monica's glasses fog up.

"Hey Mac," Della says to the skinny tattooed dishwasher.

"Good morning, Beautiful Ones," he replies. Monica grins and heads off to the bathroom where she'll finish her makeup.

"Hey Ingrid," Della calls to the head breakfast cook, who waves but doesn't turn her head. Now she's got her glittery apron, pockets filled with pens, condiments, a golf tee, and laminated pictures of Kierra; she's tying the golden sash behind her back, brushing her hand over her hair checking for stray curls. Mac says, "You're perfect," and she replies, "I know" as she brushes through

the door into the dining room. This is the Sunrise Room, one small
section of the restaurant and the most popular dining room for
breakfast. A wall of windows reveals a subtle sky, all baby pinks
and baby blues fading as the morning sun grows larger, stronger.
It's often the quietest meal of the day, when people not quite awake
murmur the headlines to each other, or simply stare out the windows. There's gratitude for coffee, and for coffee refills, the occasional grinning request for a piece of pecan pie from the lunch
menu to go with that morning coffee. Mr. and Mrs. Anderson always claim the table in the right-hand corner, a window seat, where
they hope Della will be serving them, and they are here again today.
It must be Sunday.

They watch her in silence, Mrs. Anderson with her hand to
her throat, her fingers gently clasped around her diamond 50th anni-
versary necklace as if to make it stay there, as one might hold a restless child, as if to stop time. Della, who looks like the daughter they
lost, always makes her aware of the passing time. Mr. Anderson
just watches, stiff and prim, his hands on his thighs. He watches
Della all the way to the kitchen, as if this were the highlight of his
week, this little interaction with Della. Perhaps it is. Or maybe he
just appreciates EVERYTHING these days; he's ninety, after all.
His wife is seventy-two and looks sixty. They have the money to
dress nice, and he's proud of his stock portfolio, even in these days,
making it that much easier for Mr. A. to imagine he's still 25, which,
I suppose, he is if he thinks so. I wonder if Mrs. A. feels the same
about herself? Or is that harder to do? She seems happy enough,
considering all they've been through together.

Della walks straight to their table and reads the order to
them without asking; yes, that's what they want, same as always,
except today some orange juice, because they ran out at home. Mr.
Anderson says, "It was on the list, but we forgot it and it is my
fault, it was my job to get the milk and OJ. You get to be my age,
that's what happens. And everything takes a little longer. You
make the best of it. I bent down to tie my shoes this morning, and
I said to Mrs. Anderson, 'what else can I do while I'm down here?'"
Mrs. Anderson smiles the smile of the spouse who's heard it a
thousand times already. Della laughs. "I'll be right back with your
juice."

I'm sliming and slithering through the air (feeling a bit snakelike today), grateful for the no-smoking policies, and in the morning we don't even have the candlelit tables to muddle my air with smoke and fragrance. In other words, there's less competition in the air, and I feel denser, more powerful. Sometimes, Mr. Krooms, the morning manager, cracks the windows open—that's the best, but he only does that on low air pollution days and this is not one of those. Usually I swim along just behind Della's shoulders, where I get the best view of her world. Today, though, I'm more interested in her face, so I fly a few feet ahead, constantly turning to look, to keep up with her back-and-forths, thud thud thuds through the kitchen to grab the plates, then swishy swish through the door and silent tiptoe-type steps to the customer's table, always fast and efficient, yet gentle, so mindful as she offers hot plates of eggs and waffles and biscuits and bacon without disrupting conversations, knowing that in the case of Mr. and Mrs. A. she IS the conversation, and gracefully sliding into that space for them, with them. I envy her at times, her work is so important, and she doesn't even know it. Neither does Tommy, though he values and appreciates her paycheck, and even tells her so fairly often. I have to tell you there was that time he came into the restaurant before her shift was over with a crystalline necklace in a little box in his pocket. She wore it for a week without taking it off even to sleep.

○

Tommy isn't here, this is work. Kierra isn't here, this is work. Not only that: Della left her cell phone at home again, in the morning's usual haste. Anyway, there's nothing she can do for those people right now and that worried look slowly fades as Della moves about the dining room, as she dances about in her daily career, breathes in the air of it, the water of it—she breathes in and out, in and out, like a butterfly flying, like a fish flapping her gills biding her time at the bottom of the pond, unaware of the smoke-free environment, the classical music, the hush of polite conversations. Studying her face today, I can feel her willing herself to appreciate life as it is, to count her blessings, give herself a little break from being troubled by things. She has a job that pays well; she's healthy enough to perform it; Tommy's in school; she lives in a beautiful city; and she has Kierra, who she wanted forever, who taught her what love really is. Even now the occasional cry of a babe triggers the feeling of her milk letting down, and makes her catch her breath, longing for Kierra, but then Mr. Anderson flags her down, or Josh the 16-year-old busboy asks her a question, and she's breathing again, moving, working, living her life at work.

Around 1pm she runs across the street to buy shoes for Kierra, and for lunch she eats whatever Chef Ingrid will feed her (today it's cheesy eggs and a croissant), perched on a stool with the plate on her lap, staring at the employee bulletin board.

She looks almost as fresh at the end of the day as she did at the beginning; it's been a busy one, but the customers were friendly across the board. She caught many smiles, not just from the younger men, but from women out with their daughters or friends, from elderly couples. She didn't see them all—I saw them, but she didn't consciously register them—today there were enough, enough smiles to keep her energy going. Also, she's able to leave right at 4pm, which is unusual, as her boss knows she'll say yes if asked to stay over. It's a financial issue until Tommy can finish up his school. But today, things are light by mid-afternoon, the next shift arrives on time, and she's out the door and sprinting through the parking areas with Monica to Monica's car, bouncing in, eager to pick up her own car from the mechanics, then onward to get her daughter. (Maybe they'll stop off for fast food on the way home, make time for a walk in the park.)

"Thanks for the ride, Monica, I really appreciate it."

"Bless your heart," Monica answers. "Anytime. Anytime, you just call me, hon."

Della waves, walks across the service station lot and quickly spots her car which is parked and waiting, the key under the mat. Kevin has it all fixed and ready to go, just like he said he would, and the engine sounds better than the day she bought it, used, from the Subaru place. She pulls into the daycare and parks by the play-yard fence, noting that there's a gathering of folks at the church this afternoon—she glances over her shoulder to read the portable marquee—the sign that posts the times of services and such. "Is This Church Open to All? 5PM Worship & Discussion." Long ago, Della made her decision about that question and she hasn't been back since. She beelines to Room 3, where the two-year-olds are kept from 7am to 7pm, if you need it, and again she feels grateful to be here before the sun has set.

Kierra's sitting in a corner, crying in that dry way that kids cry when they are all cried out but still need to cry. She's folded down over her lap, holding her little leg, little dry sobs mixed with old-sounding sighs, her nose all red and her lips pink, almost chapped from all the snot and tears. Della rushes to her girl and grabs her tight. Now I wish I had stayed with Kierra today, I'm torn between the two of them, I wish I could keep them both in one place.

Kierra releases a sigh of relief, then commences wailing, a fresh encore. I should have stayed with Kierra today, but I was mesmerized by Della in her golden apron, I was selfish, after all these years! In the way that I am able to know things, I know that Kierra has been crying for hours. This isn't just a temporary tantrum. It's not a sudden shriek of loneliness for her mother, it is something more important even than that, and Della knows it too, and nobody can describe what goes on just below her heart and above her stomach, knowing what she knows. But what can she do about it? Her daughter wants her, but she has to work for the health insurance, for the money. They have to eat, after all. In the absence of a solution, Della tries not to think about it too much. The less she thinks about it, the worse it will get, but she doesn't know that. If she knew, what would she do?

Miss Tracy runs over to them. "Did you get my message? I was going to call you again," she says, slightly out of breath, "but Mrs. Roberts said not to." Mrs. Roberts is the Church Secretary who switched over from running the front office to running the daycare when it opened. "She says we can't be interrupting people at work, I hope that's okay with you. I would have kept calling."

"Call me anytime," Della says, her mouth trembling... in anger? Sadness? Guilt? Half the time, she forgets her cell phone, or it's turned off, or the battery dies halfway through the day. I'm not sure what it is. It's such a strange situation, this whole daycare thing, the whole cell phone thing. I'm swirling around Della's shoulders like a shawl, petting her, comforting her, but she's feeling none of it. In fact, she appears to be shaking all over, as if she's standing outside in the snow. "I would always want you to call me if my daughter is upset like this."

"That's what I thought," Miss Tracy replies, her eyes glistening. "Kierra has been crying since lunchtime, and Mrs. Roberts said to let her cry it out," she whispers. Then in a normal tone she says, "But she didn't cry it out, she just sat there on that little chair there in the corner. I tried to console her but she wouldn't respond to me, it was like she was in a trance."

"Oh!" Della tries to gather her thoughts but they're going every which way.

Miss Tracy's whispering again. "She got out of the chair and sat on the floor, she wouldn't take her nap, or her snack-time, neither one. She says her leg hurts, but there's nothing wrong with it. I had to let her be, because we have other children here, I couldn't just sit with her all day."

Della's stammering, silently stammering. She just can't quite think. She hugs her daughter harder, tighter, feels Kierra fighting against trust, refusing to relax. Della's angry, but at the same time she is afraid of Mrs. Roberts. That old lady is so sure of her opinions, starting with her literal religious beliefs down to what time you should get up in the morning and which Christian denomination understands God correctly (hers). If Della confronts her, Mrs. Roberts might take it out on Kierra in some way. Or, Mrs. Roberts might be so offended that she kicks them out of the daycare. Then who would watch Kierra, tomorrow, when life goes on and Della has to report to work? Tommy, she can hear him complaining, "It's life, Della, just deal with it, Kierra will adjust, it'll make her stronger." Tommy is not the sentimental type, not on the surface—and I will say, his surface is pretty thick.

"I don't know what else there is...." Tracy continues. Her voice rises and fades out, like plumbing getting ready to give out. She spurts, gurgles, quits.

Della sighs. "I don't like this."

"I don't like it either. I might have to quit."

Della stares at her in surprise. "Don't—"

"Don't think ill of me. I'm sorry, but this just isn't for me. I'm going to start looking for something else."

"Could you watch Kierra?"

"Can't. I don't have a license for that."

"You don't need one, for just one kid." Della's hope surrounds her like a pink heat, you can see it in her blushing cheeks.

"I can't afford that," Tracy answers. "I need a living wage, health insurance would be nice too. Maybe you should consider staying home? You seem like you want to."

"I can't."

"Who says you can't." Tracy appears disgusted, then apologizes again, her eyes wide and bright. "I'm sorry, you should have been called. I should have called you anyway." She walks away to tend to another child. She does not look back, and now I would be crying if only I could; instead, I am the heavens breaking loose. WHO SAYS YOU CAN'T? Tommy, for one. Large cold raindrops pelt Della's shoulders as she runs to her car. She's sheltering Kierra in her arms, her angry tears mingling with my rain. We're in the car now, Della bending over her daughter, struggling with the car-seat buckles, Kierra finally fastened into her seat, her face pink and screaming.

Della's driving too fast for the conditions. Just before we reach home she veers to the left, drives up into someone's yard leaving muddy ruts in their grass as she makes a U-turn.

What's this?

Oh, of course, we're on our way to the Emergency Room, because there is something about that leg and Della is determined to be a good mother. They're going to laugh at her—no bruises, nothing broken, nothing obviously wrong. Or they'll judge her—Kierra's fussing about her leg because she needs love, she's neglected, not getting enough love. And Tommy's going to fuss about the bill. Della's making a decision without asking Tommy first, and even I am confused at first, but then a sort of knowing seeps in. It's an old, old story. I shrink back, floating near the rear window, barely resisting a timeless urge to slip up into the ethers and dissolve with the rain.

Who knew being a mother would be so hard? Who knew it would never end? I'm whispering to Della, hovering in front of Della as if to protect her as the doctor pulls the curtain aside and steps in, friendly smile, nice eyes, motherly in fact. She's telling Della not to worry, here's a prescription for antibiotics, see the pediatrician for follow-up, might want to get some blood work but no need to aggravate the child with that now. The doc has nothing useful to say about the leg pain—treat one thing at a time, she says, tell your doctor about it when you have your appointment, let him evaluate that. I would like to think that Della can feel my protective presence as she receives this disappointing information. Indeed, she seems strong as she nods, accepts the prescription with a smile and a thank you, tucks it into her purse, and begins gathering up her daughter, the diaper bag, the blankie, and herself. She's not hopeful that another Rx will do anything; this will be the fifth run of antibiotics, after all. It's 9pm, dark outside, well past Kierra's bedtime. When she steps out the ER doors into the parking lot, it's still raining, but not so hard. At home a small comfort awaits her: Tommy's made supper and he's keeping it hot for her, in the oven at 200 degrees, and she knows it will be a plate of frozen veggies, a piece of meat, and instant potatoes, enough to fill her up, but she's not even hungry, not even a little bit hungry, and she'll have to think of something else to feed Kierra, the pickiest little girl on the planet.

I'm nestled around Della's shoulders like an affectionate fur collar as she makes her way home, her squeaky worn-out wiper blades swishing hypnotically, yellow street lights flashing by in rhythm with the wipers. Kierra quit crying after two minutes in the car, plunging into sleep. After some station grazing Della turns the radio off, creating a moment of hypnotic, dark stillness, my moment to speak to her. I've been planning this for months, but unsure how to go about it, not wanting to scare her off, I've waited for something to happen that would make her tender and open enough to hear me. I touch her cheek; she lifts a hand to brush me away. I whisper into her ear—actually I am shouting, but to her it is the faintest whisper, if she can hear me at all. "Della... listen...."

"Mmmm..." she says, a sort of a tired groan.

"Della? Della?"

Nothing.

"This is your great-great-grandmother Colleen..."

Della glances over her shoulder at her sleeping child, whose head now hangs over the plastic edge of the car seat like a floppy Raggedy Ann doll. "Oof," Della says, imagining the discomfort.

"Della.... This is your grandmother.... I'm here.... Listen!"

SIX

At first I think Della is avoiding going home, when she pulls over again, even though she's just a few minutes from her house on Tryon Street. Well. I guess I am right. She sits, staring into space. Then she turns to gaze at her sleeping daughter for a while. She unbuckles herself, reaches back to rearrange her daughter's head, but it keeps flopping down. The child is hot to the touch, and suddenly Della remembers the prescription. She didn't really want to fill it. She doubts it will help. But then again. She'll have to backtrack to Walmart, the only place open this late, to get it filled, but she'd better do it now, and stock up on some more of that Children's Tylenol while she's at it.

I hurry ahead of her into the store but she's moving too fast for me, she runs right through me. She left little Kierra in the car sleeping, that's okay though, it will only take a few minutes at this time of night.... Della enters the vast bright warehouse of stuff, stuff, stuff; she zooms off to the left and I follow her, like a little trail of smoke coming off her tires. She drops off the prescription and swerves to the right, where she knows she'll find the Tylenol. She grabs that, pays for it, runs out again.

"Hey! Della!"

A middle-aged man with a grey ponytail waves to her to stop. Ach! It's Della's Uncle Ted, her mother's brother.

"Hi Uncle Ted," she replies, slowing for a moment, "How you doing?"

"Hold on Della," he says, stepping up to her and grabbing her elbow. "You gotta look what I got in my car." Close up like this, she can smell the alcohol, but as usual Ted's in a pleasant mood. Again it strikes her, how friendly he is when Kierra's not around.

"I've left Kierra in the car, I can't."

"I'm parked next to you. I saw your baby, she's fine, c'mon, you can spare one minute."

Della follows him with her ears back, she's not in the mood, but then she sees—it's a dog—and she smiles. That makes me smile too. No doubt because of Runner, and all my dogs, I'm partial to any dog I see. "Oh, Ted, he's adorable. He looks just like Kierra's doggie, do you know that? Do you remember her? Kierra named her Licky?"

"I never saw your dog."

"Well. If that's a baby he's gonna be a big dog."

A truck with an ailing muffler pulls in beside them, and I move in closer so I can hear better—seeing as I like Ted's voice, the way he sounds when he's talking about his dog.

They're looking at the pup through the passenger side window; Ted knocks on the glass and the dog looks up at them, blinking. "SHE, you mean. I'm going to train her for Search & Rescue if she's not too old for it. She's right at a year, but I agree, she has that puppy look. And she's got a nose on her all right, I've already started training her."

"How wonderful!" Della glances towards her car (it is NOT right next to Ted's—it's close, though). "You know, that dog… looks a LOT like our old dog. Oh… makes me a little sad. I wish we didn't have to give her away."

"Want to pick her up?" He's unlocking the car door.

"Wait." Now Della's in one of her stand-stills.

I see what's got her attention. There's a short, crisp-looking lady behind Della's car, writing down the license plate number.

"Wait, Ted, I'll be right back."

The lady smiles sociably when Della runs up to her, Uncle Ted following right behind (getting smack dab in my way—for a minute I can't see what's going on). Then Della & Ted can hear it, we all can hear it, Kierra crying full-out.

"Can I help you?" Della asks, wondering for a moment if the woman is a parking cop.

"You left your baby in the car," the smiling lady replies, in a strange voice, not quite stern, not quite friendly. "She's crying up a storm in there."

"I know. I can hear it. I went in to get some Tylenol for her. I have to go back for the prescription though—they're still filling it."

The lady nods sympathetically, but she doesn't move, not even a step back, as Della unlocks the car, releases her daughter from the car-seat restraint system, pulls her up and out, holds her tight to her chest. Kierra screams as Della lifts her out.

"Anything I can do to help?" the lady asks, her mouth sour.

"No. Thanks though."

"You can mind your own business," Ted says. "That would help."

"Who are you?"

"Who are YOU?" Ted retorts.

"Never mind then," the woman mumbles, stepping back, her face flushed. "All right then, I do hope she feels better."

"Thank you," Della replies, that's all she can muster. Then Ted's gone so fast that neither Della nor I see him go. I'm busy. I am pushing the nosy woman away, and she's off to her own vehicle, moving a little faster than usual because of me. There's a smell to that lady that I do not like, self-righteousness, it stinks worse than Ted's breath, I can smell it and I can feel it, that judgment that re-quires perfection in the world, insists on it, just like a dog has to have his meat. She just got a little feeding off of Della's imperfec-tion, and Uncle Ted's woundedness, and she'll be happily chewing on the bones of this for the rest of the night. Della feels it too, but she doesn't know what I know; she just takes it on, absorbs it, she's silently yelling at herself all the way back into the store, where she takes Kierra into the bathroom, sets her on the changing table, ad-ministers the Tylenol—huge, painful shriek, as if Della's killing her—then changes her diaper amid more shrieks. She gives herself hell for being a bad Mom, for working even though she doesn't want to work, for her daughter getting sick so much, she must not be getting taken care of properly, and the thoughts circle back around, she's a bad mother, her daughter is suffering, but what can she do? Thank God that snoopy, vigilante lady went back to her own car and drove off, but now another one has taken her place: a skinny fake-blond woman with a deep frown-line between her black eyebrows blows into the bathroom, puts her hands over her ears.

"She's sick," Della apologizes.

The lady nods her understanding and enters a stall. Abruptly, Kierra stops crying, but she's just gathering breath. In the interim Della can hear the blond talking on her cell phone while peeing: "Because I told you, Binkers, that's the way it is, I'm not coming home until you apologize. WHAT? Oh. Precious. Yes I want Precious, are you kidding me?"

Finally home, prescription in hand, it is going on 11pm, and every time Della tries to set her down, Kierra wakes up and cries, reaching up, clawing the air for her mother to return, so dramatic, as if she were drowning. The noise even wakes Tommy, who can snore through a hurricane. Forget sleep, everybody. Tomorrow's Monday, Della's day off, now that is something to be thankful for, she doesn't have to ask Tommy to get up and get involved, which wouldn't help anyway, because Kierra only wants Della when she's sick.

The veggies and meat slab and glob of potatoes are dry and glued to the plate when she opens the oven to see what she's got. Tommy murmurs an apology from the bedroom. "Want me to get up and get you something else?" he asks, his voice full of sleep, then he's snoring again. Della's not hungry.

"Eat, child," I whisper in her ear, but she just gets up again, pacing and rocking her baby. The idea of eating, it seems, applies to her baby, not to herself.

But I am surprised; it is almost as if Tommy heard me. He's up, grabbing that plate out of the oven, giving the potatoes a stir. "Eat," he says gruffly. "You have to eat."

Tomorrow, and nothing will get done. Della will think that she has to clean the house since she's home, but every time she gets up to start a chore, Kierra cries, demanding that Della sit and hold her throughout the day, as if she were starved for attention, insatiable, so very dramatic, whenever Della picks her up you'd think she's the old soul who's finally found an oasis after centuries of hiking through a dry desert. And she is, in her way, so Della sits. There's nothing else to do, really—anyone can see that. Even Tommy is sympathetic—not at first, but when he sees Della's face, yes, even he can see there is a problem. Arriving home at 7pm he finds the breakfast dishes in the sink, laundry basket still full, Della just sitting there on the sofa, her feet up, her hair uncombed. She spent the entire day soothing Kierra, holding Kierra, napping with Kierra.

Tommy's too tired to cook, but he's not complaining—he'll go out and find them a pizza, a bottle of red wine. All in all, then, it's a good day for Della. I want her to have endless days like this, except without Kierra being sick of course. Just be with your girl, and Tommy, just let her be with her girl. It won't last forever, it's a precious, precious time. Della has a strong motherly instinct. I wish for her to experience some true release, some recess, where she can just be with her baby until her baby is no longer a baby. That would be pure wonderfulness. That would be the right thing for everyone. Somewhere in the depths of me I need to see this happen for Della, my girl, and for Kierra, my girl's girl.

I remember my mother's arms around me so tight I almost couldn't breathe, how I could wiggle to get it just the right amount of tightness, that she adjusted to my needs on a moment-to-moment basis, the milk right there next to my cheek, warmth in abundance, sleep as needed, and my mother's eyes. She must have looked at me once, really looked at me, because I can feel her staring at me as if cutting through all my layers straight down to my original soul self, loving me there, just loving me there forever, love. Love. Love.

O

Then it all went rotten, she was gone. I remember it now, even now in my skinless, ghostly form, I have the memory of her love and the memory of my loss. My loss. Twice, it seems. It happened twice. How could that be? Did I have a twin?

I'm lying on my back under that rock. I can't move my legs, I must be sick. They are walking away from me. They have turned their backs to me. I cry outward with my whole lungs, giving it all I've got until there is no air. Then I try holding my breath, turning my head to the side, my face blue. My head rests against my right shoulder, looking away from the trail because they are gone now and I cannot bear it. I am staring instead at a wall of rock, a small dead fire pit beneath a rock overhang, a brown bird hopping about, picking through ashes. Sadly, I inhale. They must have eaten dinner here last night, but I don't remember it. I don't recall whether they fed me, but I am sick, that's why I can't remember. That's why I can't eat. I can't stomach anything. Already I am forgetting them.

Maybe I'm not human? Is that why they left me here? Maybe I am a baby bird. That's my mother over there in that fire pit, hunting me some breakfast. No, she's the river otter, a mammal mother chasing after that bird, flinging herself at the bird, standing a moment, foiled, confused as the little bird flies off. Years later I know it must have been early morning, because that's when the otter does her work, early morn, or else dusk. But now she's gone, I made the mistake, I blinked and everyone was gone, my people, and the bird, AND the otter. My only companion is the vast, clear, pristine emptiness of mountain air. The chatter of the otter was brief and businesslike; now, the silence runs so deep I can feel it in my bones. Pure silence, at first, but then I hear it, the sound I will never leave for all of my life: the creek, singing its shamanic song, laughing at its own jokes. To this day, I don't wander so far that I cannot hear a creek in the background, it's my safety zone, that sound. I close my eyes, turn inward, and pray like the mother of all mothers but even that was never enough to keep me in my body.

Sometimes I wish Della had not chosen this exact spot for her house. I was happily hermitted under that rock, slowly making my final transition, giving up, you know? Have you ever been that tired? I was like a caterpillar in a cocoon, done with being a caterpillar, on the verge of emerging. If you could see it from my eyes, you'd see yourself the bully with that bulldozer. You don't know what you are pushing out of your way to make space for yourself to sleep, eat and bathe. You have no idea what you are disturbing. You don't even know it, even you, Della, trying so hard to be good.

We did it too, in my day—we put up houses without thinking much about it.

I say build up, if you have to. Build a tree house. You shove the earth around like it's just a mess of blankets to rearrange however you like. Why not a tipi? If you have to have a big family, install bunk beds. When I realized it was Della building that house, I began petitioning her to build a smaller one, but I couldn't work out a way to get her attention. No matter what I did, she just kept on, like a zombie in a trance, like someone sleepwalking through traffic. I pounded, I screamed, I rattled the new doors off their hinges. I poured thunderstorms on them, and once, hailstones the size of acorns. I even kicked up a small tornado but it missed them completely. They just laughed and enjoyed the show. They saw it, but they didn't see it. I think it is a matter of time, really, and persistence. I hope so. You'll all be back in the tipis and glad of it.

When you are invisible you have to speak and speak and speak and speak before someone finally hears you. You can't give up. Don't give up. Eventually you will be both HEARD and UNDERSTOOD. I have not given up, but I will say I have made my peace with Della's house now that it is here.

○

Next morning baby's still holding her leg. Della's on the phone with the pediatrician but they don't have an appointment until tomorrow afternoon. Another day off, no pay. Tommy's pacing. "You sure she couldn't go on in to the daycare?" he asks. "I mean, isn't this what we pay them for? Isn't that where she got sick? It's their fault, and now they won't take care of her."

Della shakes her head, her face white. She's sipping coffee, but she's not going to eat any breakfast.

"Okay. Well, I'm late for class," Tommy says, and he's out the door. As he locks it behind him, that sound makes Della cry for some reason. I rush to the door to scold him, but what's the use, he's already in his car, it's probably good he's keeping on schedule. I turn, swirl, spin up to the ceiling, and now Della's crying hard, hugging Kierra who just cries even harder than her mother. I put my arms around her, and because I am a ghost my arms can go around and around like a long, warm blanket around her shoulders. Della reaches up with her right hand and rests her hand on mine.

Contact.

Finally.

"Della?"

She hears me. I feel her thoughts. In Della's mind's eye, she's watching her grandmother, Elizabeth Potter (my granddaughter who was born Elizabeth Hanaford, the one who ran off). I know Della hears me, because she's having a sudden memory, some odd, old memory fragment of her mother's mother—my daughter's daughter, our own Amy Ellen Elizabeth Hanaford, all right, in a blue cotton dress, weeding a garden bed, tending to those flowers she loved under the bright blue summer sky. Somewhere in the background, Elizabeth's son Ted, Cynthia's twin, a young man with curly black hair, blue eyes, home from Viet Nam going on ten years, but still not speaking much. Elizabeth's handing a flower to little Della.

Those pastel flowers she loved! Fragile, fluffy, full, like tissue flowers on a parade float, they grow like weeds for Elizabeth. "Hollyhocks," Della murmurs.

We have met in the middle.

"Yes, Della, hollyhocks! Call your mother," I say.

Della stops crying and looks up. I follow her gaze; she's studying the clock. 9am—that's 6am in her mother's time zone. Della heard me. She's picking up her phone, scrolling down to her mom's number at the end of the contact list, because for years she's been annoyed with her mother—Cynthia Elizabeth—for reasons she can't even articulate, so she lists her as "Z Mom Cynthia," the end of the list. This, even though she's loyal enough to call her mother more than just once in a while.

Grandma Elizabeth Hanaford Potter is listening too, right this very moment, I feel her crowding me. She's still alive, but with that dementia going on, she's started traveling outside her body more and more. We're both listening in on Della's phone call to her mother. Cynthia answers on the first ring, because, like her daughter, she has her phone programmed; she knows who's calling, and she only answers for Della.

"Call the doctor," Cynthia says. Elizabeth—in her spirit form, that is—she grabs at the phone, fighting me for it; she is very intense about children. "That's not right," Cynthia continues, "that leg hurting like that." Because of our bumbling, Cynthia drops the phone onto the floor.

"I did, and they don't have an appointment until tomorrow, and we've already been to the emergency room."

"What honey? I dropped the phone."

Della repeats herself.

"What did the doctors there say?"

"They said to give her the antibiotics and then follow-up with her pediatrician."

"Antibiotics don't treat leg pains."

"I know, Mom."

"Take her back to the emergency room, maybe the doctor will be awake this time."

"They'll think I'm a fanatic. They'll think I am one of those mothers who wants her kid to be sick. What's the name for that…"

"No, you're a mother, not a fanatic. Take her in, and call me when you have some answers. No, call me whether or not you get any answers. Write everything down."

"Okay. Okay, I'll go."

"Do you need me to come out there?"

"No. No, not now."

"Because I will."

"I know."

"I would drop everything. Your Grandma's in the nursing home now, and she's always said not to let her hold me back."

"I know Mom. Thanks."

"I love you."

"Love you too. I'd better go put her in the car."

"Go. I'll pray for Kierra. I'll pray for you both."

"Thanks, Mom."

SEVEN

Kierra's blue in the face from crying, but she cooperates in a limp and worn-out way, and they're back at the emergency room within the hour. Della doesn't bother with makeup, but she's got her hair combed and her underwear changed. It could be a long day. I'm a little dizzy from following that girl all over the county, but I'm keeping up, because she's listening to me now and I know she is going to need me. She's going to need her mother, too. Kierra's not yet three, she hasn't reached that critical crisis point that all my descendents go through (because of me), and it doesn't seem fair that this is happening so soon. It's not exactly a crisis… not yet… but things are not going well in the marriage and I swear, Kierra is getting sick a little too much, something is out of whack and even I don't know what it is. People think that spirits can see beyond the constraints of time, but not all of us, not me, anyway. Sometimes, yes, but always—no. Not me. Maybe that's for the higher angels. Maybe ghosts have blind spots, just like humans, things we just don't have the guts to see.

It's a different doctor. I examine her name tag: Margaret DeLap, MD. I examine her face: she looks kind. She seems concerned. "Hm," she mumbles softly. " According to the chart…..It looks…. It looks like…. You were just in here the other day?"

Suddenly, there is eye contact.

"It's okay," I shout into Della's ear. "She isn't judging you for coming back to the Emergency Room." Della hears a faint whisper, more like a thought, saying IT'S OKAY, and that's all it takes. She pours out the story like snow melting off a mountain, and Dr. DeLap is nodding and listening, and finally she says, "Let's admit her. We'll do some tests, a diagnostic admission. She's got a couple of bruises this morning. We'll have her out in a day or two.

Sometimes you never find out what it was, but we'll look as hard as we can."

"Thank you," Della stammers, too relieved to be frightened.

Days later I am still draped about my Della's shoulders light as silk. We've shared some conversations and some dreams, and we're actually becoming friends. Amy Ellen Elizabeth is the cornerstone for our communication, the embodiment in Della's dreams and daydreams that speaks my voice—or is it Elizabeth's voice?—to our shared offspring Della. I'll bet you didn't know that those old ladies with Alzheimer's are still active, still tending their flocks by night. You might not know how strongly grandmothers claim their granddaughters, what barriers they overcome in the process, but we do, we know. We are mightily attached, even from a distance like Seattle. We're like a string of beads, each one strengthening and lengthening the necklace until the story can't be broken and won't end. We might be cranky or soft, but we're always beautiful and always in love. Don't doubt it, even if you have the nastiest grandmother you ever met, she is still a bead in the chain and without her the chain is broken. You don't have to talk to her, but know her. Somehow, find a way to know her. Amy Ellen Elizabeth (I like the sound of her three names, even though we call her Elizabeth)—she's the soft type, the lover type, whose lap you could rest your head in any time of the day or night, whose hand is always warm, who looks at you with eyes that see. Elizabeth didn't see her daughter Cynthia so well, no she did not, in spite of all her intentions, and that's part of the reason she has the dementia now, because of all the things she couldn't stand about her life, including the fact that Cynthia ended up a single mom who barely had time for her own daughter. And Ted in Viet Nam: She could not stop that. You see, even when we mess up, our hope is for the next generation to do a little better, feel a little better, find a bit more happiness. Even though we mess up, the connection is there, strong as the healthiest heart, bigger than any one mother-daughter relationship. It is a whole world, it's not just two people.

You see, again, let me explain, in case it's hard to follow. I am the grandmother of Amy Ellen Elizabeth, and Amy Ellen Elizabeth is the grandmother of Della. This is how we are able to speak to each other, and that's the best I can explain this part of it. Sorry if you still don't understand. It's mother love, except, it's grand—

GRANDmother love. There's slightly more magic and mystery in it, if you can imagine that. We grandmothers can criss-cross many dimensions to find each other, not being stuck in this one world that you are so committed to at the moment. In case you think this means that Amy Ellen Elizabeth is dead, like me, think again. As I've already told you, she's in another sort of in-between. She is not a ghost, but she has had Alzheimer's for three years now. She weighs only a few pounds, and she wonders about, wanders about, in pajamas that go over your head so you can't unbutton them. On her better days, she thinks Grandpa Potter's still living in the old family cottage and the nursing assistants get very sentimental about that. I suppose with a marriage that lasted 40 years you might cling on forever, you might hold onto anything, even the ghost of a memory. I never had that experience, my Thomas dying off so young. I haven't walked in those particular moccasins.

These days my Elizabeth floats about six inches above her body, aware of everything and nothing, even though her fleshy brain has just about stopped remembering anything except holly-hocks and tiny black-haired babies.

As for me, I'm growing; I will remain a strong SILK scarf around my Della's shoulders and I'm growing longer and longer, layering her with my protective presence, and she listens when I say, "Go for a walk down the hall," or "Get yourself some of that grape juice, not coffee. Juice." She listens when I say, "Just tell Tommy that everything will be okay," so that his anxiety doesn't ripen and burst into a temper fit, and that does seem to help, just reassuring him and not asking him to help, not asking him for support. The point is not to be in charge of his wellbeing, it's just that his wellbe-ing affects her, every minute of her life. And I'm not telling her to leave Tommy, because I know how hard it is to raise a child alone. Sometimes she says, "I *am* raising Kierra alone," but she doesn't realize, she doesn't know. Tommy plans the budget, mows the grass, sleeps in the same bed with her every night, snoring. He builds her up about the same amount that he tears her down. There is a balance there, for the moment. I can see that it's tolerable, if only barely. And she has no one else, with her mom so far away, and her uncle—well, for now Ted's just a problem.

Della must figure out how to be stronger inside herself, and that's where I come in. I am here to chase the orphan out of her, then she'll be unstoppable. It won't be about Tommy anymore, what he does or doesn't do. It won't be about her mother's grief as a single mom, and it won't be about pleasing her boss at the restaurant. It's about mothers being free to protect their children, which is a freedom: that is, it can't be given or earned. You heard me.

Before you know it the weekend is upon us, with a heavy work schedule for Della. She's promised to return to work Friday afternoon, for the dinner shift. Friday morning, she's checking Kierra out of the hospital. Kierra's little leg seems better, for no apparent reason. Her fever's nearly gone, and the congestion seems to be under control. She's got a Tuesday appointment with her regular doctor to discuss the test results, and that's good timing because Della already has that day off. I'm zooming through traffic with Della now, sometimes taking the wheel—she lets me, briefly, without realizing she's doing it—and we are like a team, almost, except that I can see her better than she sees me.

She's really quite talkative if you don't interrupt. She has a lot on her mind. She wants out of the marriage, but she sees no way to do it. She thinks Tommy would die if she left, he'd be so helpless you see. Well. She is beginning to realize that SHE might die if she stays! I just listen. She has to make the decision, but she doesn't have to make it alone. She really doesn't. She is surrounded by women who love her—me (the mother of all ghosts, I sometimes like to say), and her grandma Elizabeth, and her mom Cynthia—even Kierra, a little mother herself even at two years old. The thing is, once you have kids you can't overlook the men. In all my experience I don't know much about that part, but anyone can see that Tommy's a kind of static on the psychic line.

You can't overlook the children, either. My Della's in a tight spot all right.

Della flings herself back into her work, relieved that she has done something about her daughter, but frazzled down to her stem with Tommy's reaction to the potential medical bill. He thinks the admission was unnecessary, the tests excessive. He blames Della for being too weak to refuse the admission. He blames the doctors for being greedy. He blew up right before she went to work today and she had to leave Kierra with that fussing baby of a man without knowing when he might calm down. If she's going to leave him, she's going to have to keep her job. If she leaves her baby with him while she works, who knows. Will he even watch her, or will he leave her in the playpen crying while he plays his video games? If her mother comes to help, her mother will see the problems and be upset, and then Della will be worrying about her, too, feeling judged on top of everything else. IT'S NOT THAT BAD, MOTHER. I hear the whole thing, she's been thinking very loudly ever since the first visit to the emergency room. Like I said, I don't say much. It's not time for that. Orphans need to be listened to for a long, long time before you can tell them anything.

Yes, I understand, I'm listening—you're telling me that Della is not an orphan. But she is, and that is because of me. Stick with me and I will make it clear to you, until you are able to understand that you are an orphan too. Stop reading now if you don't want it.

O

Della's gotten her hours all switched around because of being off with Kierra. Saturday night, she returns home energized from a busy evening of big tips and happy customers, and Tommy's forgotten his outburst. He's making a website for his latest idea about selling dirt, so he ignores Della when she comes in. Kierra's sleeping peacefully in the middle of their bed, and her diaper is dry. They even have sex the next morning, as if to push the re-set button. It works, for a few hours, and they sip coffee together without conflict.

Maybe things will just even out over the course of the years, the many years to come. Marriage is a long, long thing. Its dreariness is something all are familiar with; its joys, so I have heard, come more often toward the end, after the kids are grown, when the grandchildren begin arriving. Della—being Della—used to push it with Tommy. She wanted more. She persuaded Tommy to see a counselor, a fellow named Goody Tripp, I think that was his name. In a private meeting with Della, Goody persuaded her he could cure an alcoholic in three sessions. Well! Tommy does not regard himself as an alcoholic, and he's right, that is not his problem. So what happened? Tommy and Goody became friends, that's what happened.

Sure, Tommy stopped drinking for a few weeks, that was easy seeing as he wasn't addicted to it. But three months later Della found them in the bar together, Tommy and Goody, having a good time. Now when she fights with Tommy, she mentions the "alcoholic alcohol counselor" in her most sarcastic voice, but it has no effect on Tommy, because Tommy won, and he knows it. Tommy wins by out-yelling or out-lasting the other person. Nowadays she just sets it all aside. Instead of arguing with Tommy or trying to understand him (or heaven forbid HEAL him), she sets it aside and her mind bends just a little bit more off its center. She forgets, finally. Whatever it is (she's forgotten), she doesn't bring it up. She has a larger concern now: Survival. Making enough money to support the three of them during the times when Tommy needs to follow his heart, or when he's too depressed or anxious or high to look for work. Right now, things are relatively good in those three areas and I'm coaching her on how to keep it that way, for her own sake, that's all, her own wellbeing.

That's right, honey, walk on eggshells, all the way out that door.

Tuesday starts out sunny, and I head out to the doctor with Della, enjoying her cheerful heart. Kierra's fussy but not beside herself, still a little warm but eating and drinking sufficiently. She seems on the mend. I take a little break to fly above the roof of the car, feel the wind in my face, take in the sunshine that cannot burn my skin. The wind flows through me, through my eyes, nose and mouth, out the back of my shadowy skull, tickling my spine. Della parks and removes Kierra from her locked-in position, that four-point restraint. (How do people stand these things?) Me, I feel fortunate in comparison, grateful to be so light and so free. I don't even have thoughts, most of the time, just wind whistling through the place where I once had a fleshy brain with a thick stubborn skull standing watch over it, "protecting" it, keeping all those thoughts from escaping, all those grand ideas, like Kierra herself trapped in that car seat wiggling to get out.

Dr. Bailey greets Della with his usual smile, but there's concern in his eyes as she settles into a chair, Kierra on her lap. I see it first, and my reaction is so intense, clouds begin to form in the skies above us. They come in fast, low, and thick, as Dr. Bailey says that word, leukemia, and that's about all that Della can take in. It is a certain type, she can't make it stick in her mind, but she thinks what he is telling her is that it is not necessarily a good type to have but it could be worse, she is able to hear that but not in his careful medical terminology. What she hears is: leukemia, but a slower, more chronic form? She asks this, but she still can't hear his answer. He's writing the words down for her on a blank prescription, and he sees Kierra watching him, so he makes a smiley face at the bottom of the paper. Kierra smiles. Della bursts into tears. I am comforting her with all the grandmothers I can muster up; through me, all the female generations wrap themselves about her, but she can't feel us, she can't feel a thing.

I'm outraged. I haven't been this angry since they laid me down on that dirt and walked away. I am bursting out of my sinewy spidery self straight up through the ceiling and out into the sky, shooting straight up through the thick overlay of clouds above us. I look down at the cotton carpet of clouds and scream so loud that a jet, passing above, breaks the sound barrier. I know what's going to happen, I know, I know. By the time Kierra is three.... I am not going to say it.

Oh hell. What do I know? Patterns change. Patterns die out. That's what I've been sticking around for, to see that fire finally go out. It will. I have been there, done that, it need not be repeated ever ever ever ever. Up above the clouds I am splitting into a million tiny pieces of white cottony dust that sparkles as it floats down into the clouds, I have become a rainmaker, tickling the clouds until they give up their weightlessness and return to water which is vengeful in its release. Driving home, Della can barely see through the rain on her windshield and the tears in her eyes which she keeps gulping back, because why be sad about something unknown? Why cry now? That might bring it on, the thing she fears.

That's what I say. We're thinking in tandem. Scary, sure, but no matter how scary it might be, the future is completely unknown, even to me. It will be all right. That's what I say as I tuck Della and Kierra into bed that night. Don't try to know it, don't make up scary stories, don't even think about it. No point in it. I murmur the ancient salve, "It's going to be all right. Get some sleep." To my delight, Della, her cheek against the pillow, her hand on Kierra's head, utters the very same words.

EIGHT

Next morning, Della is ready for my next instruction mostly because she ignored my first one—she didn't sleep a wink last night. Her mind is now putty. She's sitting at the kitchen table gulping coffee and scribbling in her journal, so I take the pen and force her to spell out the words: "Call mother and ask her to come." She stops, suddenly sleepy, looking at what she just wrote with a quizzical expression. Then she's overcome with drowsiness, now that the sun is just peeking up, spilling in through a crack in the curtains. There goes her head, she's asleep on the table next to a half cup of undrunk coffee that is cooling fast.

As if she can sense that Della is finally feeling the call of sleep, Kierra begins to whine, just a little, then louder, then louder. Mamama...... mama... mamama... mama.... mamama..... Della opens her eyes, closes her eyes, then opens them, then picks up her cell phone, steps outside onto the back porch, calls Cynthia. From somewhere in some inside pocket she pulls out a cigarette—I'd not seen her smoke before this—and spills out the entire story to her mother, including her concerns about Tommy, which she'd always withheld as she felt, somehow, ashamed. Her husband is a reflection on herself, I suppose that's what she's been thinking. But now she has a real emergency on her hands. She just doesn't see how Tommy can help with this—he really doesn't have an ounce of motherliness in him. So her mother will come. She will! Cynthia's already on her way; when all is said and done that bond persists, maybe it'll grow now, who knows. Don't ever think you know something once and for all, because things are twisting and turning all the time in every direction. For example, it's a good thing Cynthia is coming, because two hours later, after Tommy's out of the bathroom and she's told him about the diagnosis over a cup of strong coffee, and after he kicked the side of his car for no apparent reason before driving to work (didn't he say he'd be off today?), another unexpected thing happens. Two strangers in very nice suits materialize on her front step knocking on the door, and she ignores them because she is sure they are Jehovah's Witnesses, but they won't be ignored, and it turns out they are Mr. Pearson and Ms. Jones, come to interview her about some parenting complaints, some concerns about "that alcoholic person" in the Walmart parking lot, and Kierra's apparent fear of her own mother, and something in addition to that incident going on in the bathroom of the Walmart on that very same night. There were TWO witnesses, TWO complaints.

If they get a chance to talk to Tommy they'll have their home run, so it is a good thing he went to "work."

Mr. Pearson says, "She screamed when you picked her up, according to the witness."

"She was in pain."

Ms. Jones says, "We got a report. So we have to investigate that. You understand."

"I didn't hurt my daughter."

"That's believable," says Ms. Jones. "But you understand, if there is a report, we have to investigate. Do you have records?"

"Records?"

Ms. Jones leans forward. She can see that Della is somewhere else, in some sort of fog, another sign that there could be abuse going on in this home. "You know, hon, like a doctor's visit."

"Oh yes, of course. That's where we were that night, at the emergency room, and I was filling a prescription, that's why we were out so late."

"That'll help. You know, though," says Ms. Jones, "Sometimes it is not so much about you, but about your support system, or in other words, the other people who might have access to the child? Is the father in the home?"

"Yes, my husband lives with us." Della's indignant now, despite her misgivings and complaints about Tommy.

"Why wasn't he watching the baby while you filled the prescription? You couldn't take the baby home? Maybe he could have gone out to get the medicine while you put her to bed?"

Della's speechless; Tommy was sleeping, that's why, and she
didn't want to wake him up because he would be grumpy and mean
about it. She's shaking her head, but no words can make it out, she
can't speak at all. Her mind is freezing up. Her husband should be
helping her, it's true, and she's so ashamed about that (that she
could pick someone who doesn't care about her, and keep on living
with him) that she can't even think about it, much less admit it. He
has the potential, to be sure. He would help her, maybe, if he
wasn't high, or asleep, or on the computer, or hanging with his
sleazy friends. He would help her, maybe, if she beat him with a
whip. It's true. That time she threatened to divorce him, he made
an extra effort for a full week. But now, she's adjusted to it; he
mows, he works, he balances the checkbook. He changes the oil.
She's too busy working so they can live paycheck-to-paycheck to
give it any serious thought. She's stuck with it. He just doesn't
know how to love, that's all. Or it could be that he loves, but
doesn't know how to express it, that's what his mother said.

I'm pushing the social workers out of Della's living room.
It takes everything I've got, but finally they both stand up at once,
extend their hands, shake Della's with warmth and smiles, looking
at each other with confused expressions. They really don't know
what to make of this, everything seems okay. There'll be a doctor's
appointment, a formal evaluation, another home visit, and possibly
a psychological evaluation for the parents if it goes that far. "I
doubt that it will," says Mr. Pearson. "I don't think you have anything to worry about."

Della closes the door behind them and locks it. "Tommy is
going to flip," she says to me. "I won't let him," I answer. Again,
she hears me, she just doesn't know exactly who I am, and that's
okay, sometimes I am not sure either.

"Great, now I'm talking to myself," she says, plopping
down on the sofa beside Kierra who is content for the moment,
picking her nose.

O

Tommy doesn't come right home that night. He doesn't
call. Cynthia, Della's long-lost mother, arrives first, pulling her
worn brown suitcase behind her, dropping her paisley travel bag on

the kitchen table, pulling out boxes of candy and toys and bath oil beads before she even gives her daughter a hug. She is so anxious that the air hums and I feel a little seasick from all the up and down activity, until Della offers a glass of wine and things begin to settle. Cynthia is my granddaughter's daughter, and I know what happened to her when she was three. She managed to forget, but to this day she can't sit still. Well that's not so bad in the overall picture of life, is it? Not being able to sit still? Cynthia did get married, later in life. Before that she had little Della, and to her great credit she put food on the table and made it to most of Della's school events in the evenings. And when Della finally demands a hug, her mother can give one.

"Where's Tommy?" says Cynthia, after the hug. "Where's Kierra?"

"I don't know where Tommy is, but Kierra's on our bed sleeping. Go look, I covered her up with the quilt you made for her."

"You're using it? Wonderful!" her mother says, nervous, as though Della might bop her on the head at any moment.

"Of course we use it, it's Kierra's favorite." Della smiles kindly at her mother, wanting her mother to feel wanted, at least for now.

"Wonderful," says Mom, "don't mind if I do," and she's off to the bedroom, no more word about Tommy, for which Della is thankful.

Some things haven't changed. Her mother still walks with her head bent down like she's walking into a hailstorm, even in the house. And she TALKS unevenly, lunging forward and jerking backward, like she doesn't quite understand how to use the clutch.

There's another knock at the door, which causes Della to jump. She's been jumpy lately around Tommy, and fearing the sound of her phone ringing, and that was BEFORE social services showed up on her doorstep disguised as Jehovah's Witnesses. Who can you trust. She sighs her relief when she sees it is only her Uncle Ted, who's not been by the house to visit in months, maybe a year. She's supposing he's come by because he saw her at the store the other night, which jogged his memory that she exists. There is something sweet about him, once you get used to the smell of alcohol. He doesn't wait for her to open the door, but tries to walk right in, as he always does, wherever he goes, that hint of alcohol and the lopsided smile preceding him like his personal invitation, his season's pass. But the door's locked. "DELLA!" he yells, in his best imitation of Marlon Brando. "DELLA! OPEN UP!"

She's already opening the door.

"Where's my SISTAH!" he exclaims. "I heard she was here."

"How'd you know?"

"She told me, silly, she's my sister after all." He gives Della a big smooch on the lips followed by a generous hug.

"Of course. Silly me."

He's walking straight through her kitchen to the bedroom in the back of the house, and she hears his shouts, his loud exclamations of love and the inevitable musical (vocal) performance in which he imitates that musician from Detroit, his hero, Bob Seger. "You're still the same, da-da-da-da-da-da-da, you're still the same, some things never change, you're still the same, da-da-da-da-da-da-da." He wakes Kierra, of course, who joins in with her own wails. She's terrified, or mad, sometimes it is hard to tell which. Della comes running. I'm trying to figure out my place in this mess, what's a ghost to do, all these large dense living bodies swishing about, thrashing unproductively like rhinos in a muddy river, emitting loud noises, puffing cigarette smoke from their nostrils, scaring the little fairy child who probably weighs what, twenty pounds at the most? No wonder childhood is a nightmare. I'm weightless and I have barely begun to succeed in communicating with Della, only during quiet moments at that. I feel utterly helpless now, and it pains me to see Della, who is working on becoming middle-aged herself, struggling with these slightly older middle-aged goofs who are not helping her out much, in fact, at the moment, are only adding to her troubles. Ted's picked Kierra up and he's running, unsteadily, to meet Della, flinging the baby into Della's arms so fast and so hard that Della nearly falls over. Instead she lands, sitting on the sofa, Kierra bursting into laughter—it's the roller coaster effect, works every time—until she remembers she's mad, and she cries again, louder, but less convincing this time.

Later, Della will say to me, "they over-react to everything," and that captures this moment. They're on pins and needles all the time, in addition to being drunk, or, in Cynthia's case, on Xanax, or both. You'd think those things would calm them down. To be honest, young reader? There's too much water under the bridge for any of these people to cope with, so in case you're feeling lonely, you've got plenty of company. I wouldn't blame Della if she cursed me for suggesting she call her mother, but I also wouldn't take it back. Okay, okay, to be honest it was not a suggestion, it was a motherly command, a desperate motherly command, and I couldn't help placing it into her mind at that exact moment when I did it, subliminally and predictably, as if a gene had been switched on, because it is time for the shit to hit the fan, as Tommy likes to say. If you didn't know it, DNA is a generational thing, it was never designed for just one lifetime, just one person. Della's bloodline is just now entering its adolescence—that's one way to put it—but in a good way, we can only hope.

Because I'm a "mere" ghost, I own nothing. Just the Great Love keeps me alive—I don't eat, drink, eliminate, shiver, or sleep. I don't even own vocal chords, which means I can't talk or sing. I don't exactly think, either, because there's no fleshy brain to contain thoughts, to fire off all those infinite tiny chemical-electrical explosions, to dream dreams and daydream daydreams. At the moment I am glad of it, because Della and her people just look clumsy, tired, heavy. If you could see them right now, you wouldn't envy them either, even though their house looks good from the curb and they keep their cars clean. I wouldn't want to change places, even when Kierra finally settles down in Della's arms, casting offended looks at her grandma and great-uncle, and Ted exclaims, "I shouldn't've thrown the baby. I have NEVER got that pass down," referring to his quarterbacking days, and Cynthia smacks him, hard, on the arm, making Kierra laugh again. Even Della smiles.

Having a body entails a lot of action, which some people enjoy, but I have always preferred my place here in the ethers where I can see almost everything and there's no need for sleep, for dreams or nightmares, for social conversation and manners. Now I just shake my head, so to speak, I swish back and forth in the night air, a little restless, uncertain what to do next. I follow the trail of smoke from Ted's freshly-lit cigarette, briefly wanting one for myself, and then, for a few minutes, I AM the cigarette smoke, mmmm, and then I am gone out the window with Ted's smoke. Gone looking for something.

Della looks up. She feels my sudden absence, it feels like a sudden shame. Which becomes a blush. I tell her, I'll be back.

The crisp night air is indigo above me, and black and damp beneath the trees. I'm under my rock overhang, listening to the creek. There's movement, some small being making her way to Della's back door, as if compelled, as if there would be shelter there, or food, something worth hunting, worth sniffing out. A raccoon? Possum? What is it? It's an old being, something from before this house, exuding some kind of wisdom that speaks a non-human dialect and puts out a scent. For a moment I swear it's that little girl, it's ME... confused, still trying to find my mother in this very house, taking advantage of the time warp to finally come home. Nothing frightens me, not even a ghost of myself, but I do float up to give it room, whatever it is. I'm separate from it, which is unusual as I don't normally differentiate all that much between myself and other life; I could breathe myself in and out of her hot solid body if I wanted, but her body is not exactly hot, not exactly solid. Is she sick? Is she simply alone? Did she die out there, under that rock? I begin to wonder, was I completely lost at three? Was everything that came after just a made-up story? No. How could I have had a child, and lived on in the afterlife to watch generations of my own offspring, my own brown-haired girls dancing, advancing like an unstoppable hot current beneath the thin clear waters of time?

Whoever it is, this awkward being is not dead, not a ghost, but she's desperate, determined to have her say about herself, to tell the world her indignation. Ah, I see now, as I allow myself to float in a little closer: Her little face is like Kierra's, tired of the drama already, offended but amused at the same time. It's a soft, furry little face, with round, unblinking childlike eyes. It must be me, some incarnation of me, not quite materialized but more than a mere dream, toddling and crawling along the dark and uneven path that leads directly from my rock to the back door of Della's house. She's determined in her search, she is me, back then, still searching, as if she could claim Della for her own mother and finish whatever it was we started more than a century ago. She's not a selfish little girl, this being; she does have a mission, I can see that. If she's bound to find a good mother for herself, there's some higher purpose in it. When one is helped, all are helped.

The back door is locked against her. I circle back to my rock for any other clues, and sure enough, the fire pit is glowing, and footprints all around, tiny footprints, nothing else. When I return, she's still standing at the back door, reaching for the doorknob, but she's become something else, or are my eyes deceiving me?

Yes, that is a full-grown river otter, not a child at all, not a ghost, not me. Did she shape-shift? Maybe it was a river otter all along? ...The way she toddled through the shadows with such a childlike grace... I'm flummoxed, and amused. She's slinking under the house—they are good hiders, otters, very skillful at disappearing. I played hide-and-seek with one in my raggedy youth— Runner flushed it out, chased the otter from our creek all the way back to the big river, and I ran all the way down there with them, jumping into the river, and swimming, for only a few twinkling minutes, with that marvelous playful sprite. Her head would sink beneath the water, then pop up 10 yards away, only to vanish again, here and there all around me, her round head popping up, then disappearing, until finally I lost her completely. I'm sure she watched me from some concealed vantage point as I scrambled onto the steep bank, shook myself off, wandered back up the trail and out of sight.

Oops, look. There's a man standing under the trees up above the house, lighting a cigarette, watching the movements in the kitchen with some interest. Why is everyone smoking? I can't quite make out who he is, but he seems friendly, relaxed. Here we all are, but who exactly are we? A man in the shadows behind the house, an otter beneath it, a ghost (me) by the back door, and that cute little family—my people—inside, watching T.V. and drinking cocoa. And smoking.

For now, I'll hover back and forth from my rock to the back door of the house, watching the fire slowly die, the footprints disappear with the evening wind. It's a memory, a mirage, that fire. I'll replay in my mind: Little girl/otter stumbles along my path, she leans against the door, reaches up for the back-door latch, then slides like a snake under the house. I could choreograph it, a twilight version of Salute to the Sun for the elementals. Walk, Lean, Reach, Slide. Walk, Lean, Reach, Slide.

What I want is for that River Otter to come back out. Walk, Lean, Reach, Slide, RETURN TO ME. I feel like I know her, and if not, I would LIKE to know her. I have seen her stubborn, child-like intention clearly—she intends never to move—I do understand that. I've only just come out from three decades under my rock, myself. I do understand, and I finally give up this meditation of Otter-Watching. It's time for action. Circling back to the present moment, exactly where I left off, I'm floating on a cool night-air current that flows under the house, following that otter into the crawl space and up through that hole between the walls and now I've found my way back into the house, into a bright kitchen with Della, Kierra and Cynthia. My otter is nowhere in sight, but this is even better. I love to be INSIDE a house at night, the artificial light, T.V. flashing bright colors every half-second, the smell of chocolate everywhere. It's amazing, how bright and warm it feels, how incongruent with the deep hazel night air just on the other side of these walls. I forget about the otter. Uncle Ted's lying on the floor, singing a song about sailboats, tapping the beat with his cowboy boot against a leg of the kitchen table.

NINE

"So where were you?" Della's saying, and I start to answer but Cynthia answers for me. Della's not even talking to me. After all these decades I still forget that I'm invisible, and I actually feel a twinge of hurt, because I know that when Della really pays attention, when there aren't other beings around to distract her, she truly "sees" me, so to speak. Just now, I feel ignored, and I do not like it.

"Everywhere," Cynthia says.

"That's vague, Mom."

"Yes, it is, honey. I know," Cynthia replies. "What I mean is, I couldn't settle down. It was the times I guess. I'm sorry. Your dad couldn't make up his mind back then, and I guess neither could I. We were restless, young and immature." She sighs. "His beard grew a foot long at one point, he said he was saving money on razors, but he was spending what he saved on pot, you know. You know that by now."

"I knew that when I was ten."

"You were still going over there when you were ten?"

"I was twelve the last time I saw him."

"Ach, my memory. Well he had a rough life, and by now I forgive him. It's harder to forgive him walking away from you, though. You forgive someone for hurting you, yourself, that makes sense to me. But how do you forgive someone for hurting someone you love? For hurting your own child? I still don't know, I don't think I'm ever gonna know. I guess I did my share of hurting—"

"Don't start…"

"You're right."

"It's okay, Mom, don't worry about it, it all worked out. It's good you never got married to each other. But I was wondering where we lived when I was born, and you were gone for a while, when was that? I remember it. Sort of. What happened?"

Cynthia stands up and peers out the window. "I heard something," she says. She doesn't want to talk about the time she went into the hospital when Della was not much older than Kierra, only three, to be exact.

"Oh, it's just Tommy. Tommy's out there behind the house," Ted says. "I saw him up there when I was coming in. He's afraid of you, Cynthia."

There's a harsh knock on the front door. "That must be him," Della says, "but I didn't hear his car."

"Why's he knocking on his own door?" Ted asks, raising his thick eyebrows in delighted wonderment.

"Because it's not him," Ted answers himself, as Della opens the front door to Mr. Pearson and Ms. Jones. They've returned, this time with a police officer, and the moon up over their heads, rising fast now. Butner, the dog next door, is howling all by himself even though this neighborhood is full of dogs, and with the moon and all it's a lonely sound.

"Sorry to bother you at night," says Mr. Pearson, "but we got a call that there was a disturbance here, some kind of racket, baby crying. I'm sure it's nothing, your baby being sick and all. But because there's already been a complaint on you we had to come on out. We brought Officer Trantham with us, but that's just the protocol when we have to come out at night."

"Come in," Della says. "Nothing's going on. I'm not sure why they would have called, or who would have called. I know you can't tell me."

"We can't say."

"Come in. Have some hot chocolate."

The officer follows the social workers into the house, bowing his head politely as he steps over the threshold. His eyes rest on Ted, with a look of bright recognition, but he doesn't say anything—even when Ted salutes to him—just swallows and continues to the kitchen where Della's offering a seat. "Thank you, Ma'am," he says. "That's kind of you," he says, as she pulls a box of cookies out of the cupboard and arranges them on a plate. He's nice enough to take one, even though some of his superiors would advise against it, even though his wife wants him to lose 10 pounds.

"So could you go get your baby and let us see her?" Ms. Jones asks, as she and her partner sit down beside Trantham.

"Yes of course, she just fell asleep." Della knows not to let on that she sleeps with Kierra every night, that the crib is just decoration, a place to stash the baby for two minutes while Della gets dressed in the morning, that she believes babies should be slept with until at least age three, if not four. I support that. It's protective, you see. But some people in Della's day and time are as crazy about that as they used to be about breast feeding, they think the more you act like a mammal, the lower you are, and sometimes they enforce those ideas with the law if they can crack your door open, get a foot into your business. Della's in the bedroom trying to pick up her daughter without waking her, Cynthia following her nervously, adding to everybody's anxiety, while the officials wait at the kitchen table, the social workers making chit-chat to try to soften things. Officer Trantham ignores them. He raps his knuckles against the table, studying Uncle Ted. Uncle Ted is sitting up now, but he's still on the floor. "I've got that low blood," he says in explanation, when he sees that Officer Trantham is overtly observing him. "I get dizzy if I stand up too fast."

"You mean low blood pressure?" Trantham asks, conversationally.

"Yeah that, where you faint easy if you stand up too fast. But no matter, y'all aren't here to talk to me anyway. But you can if you want—"

Ms. Jones is mouthing the word "drunk" to her colleague, when her eyes suddenly widen and she screams—"OHMYGOD WHAT-IS-IS-IS-IS-THAT?????"

Della drops her baby back on the bed, as gently as she can, but it's too late, she's woken the child. She rushes out of the bedroom.

A muscular, grey rat-looking creature is peeking out at the little gathering from the bathroom door at the far end of the living room, and at the sound of screaming, it bolts across the floor, across Ted's legs, and scrabbles frantically at the front screen door until the flimsy latch yields and the animal escapes. Only Della and I can see that it's a river otter, not a rat, as improbable as that may seem to you—not that it makes much of a difference in the minds of County Officials. Only Tommy knows about the open space behind the bathroom linen closet where a piece of the wall board didn't fit straight, and he took it off a couple months ago thinking he'd replace it, but none of that matters now, with a live wild animal frolicking through the house, running loose. It could have rabies, after all.

Kierra, half awake and half asleep, calls out, "mamama... ma... mamama...." And reaches out for her mother, who was, after all, just there, wasn't she? Picking her up? Dropping her back down onto the bed? She rolls over once, twice, and falls onto the floor, a heart-stopping WHOMP before the inevitable scream. Because her leg already hurts, because she's still running a fever, the scream is piercing, the type of scream that gets immediate results.

Later, much later, it's funny to imagine a river otter finding her way into someone's bathroom, searching for water? But tonight it means another trip to the emergency room for x-rays, and emergency foster care for Kierra. Ted can't stand this sort of thing. He rushes out of the house as soon as those white-faced authorities have left with his grand-niece. He rushes out like he's going to vomit, which he does, out of sight of the women. A mile down the road, Ted's picked up at the corner of Church Street and Hayward Road, another DUI and this time driving without a license, and no doubt when Kierra's social service case is reviewed it'll be noted that a drunk was hanging out at the house along with a river rat, yes, the largest rat they'd ever seen. The judge won't believe it was an otter, and anyway, how much difference is there, when it comes to wild animals in the house with an unsupervised baby who has cancer, who is allowed to fall out of bed... and are all those five, count them, FIVE, bruises really caused merely by the cancer?

This could be seen as a defeat in so many ways, but it is actually the start of something. I have to believe that or I would disappear into thin air, I would be done once and for all, and the timing is not right for that to happen. I can't leave while they have that big heavy house on my property, right next door to my rock, where I was resting with more and more contentment as the decades streamed by. I want that house gone, to be honest. I won't be able to sleep as long as they are there, so I figure they must still need me for something, though my heart—if I had one—is heavy, so to speak. My heart is heavy with my knowledge of the past, which makes me fear the future. It's my fault. If I had not been an orphan… I can't give that to Della, that legacy. I have to find something new for her, or I might as well give up my rock and just become a gypsy ghost, purposeless, but free. Let the house stay there until it, or my rock, slides down the mountain; or until MY rock and THEIR house both slide down that steep hill together.

○

I won't describe the weeping. When it goes on and on like that it becomes boring. Della's barely able to think, but she has to go to work or the social service people will accuse her of not being able to provide for her child. Tommy watched the whole thing from the trees up behind the house—good judgment on his part. He's not stupid. Della just didn't know—she will soon—how much pot he smokes. She thinks it's cigarettes, but he uses the cigarettes to cover up the pot smell. Maybe someday she'll come to understand he was smoking it all along, pretty much every day, since before they ever met, because it's the best thing he could find for that painful feeling he gets in his chest and that emptiness in his stomach that only goes away if he stuffs it with food. For now, though, she's crying, as if that would help. Her mother's finally gone to bed, although it's almost morning; she turned out all the lights and left Della to cry herself to sleep, but Cynthia isn't sleeping either. She's staring at the ceiling, cursing Della's AWOL father and craving a cigarette even though she quit that twenty years ago. She's in bed without brushing her teeth or washing her face, because she forgot to pack a toothbrush and she couldn't find a clean washcloth, and she didn't want to ask Della for anything, not now. It's her fault, she knows it in her bones, but she's run out of remedies for what happened in the past. It's her fault that she didn't protect Della enough, that she wasn't there enough when Della was growing up. She might have asked more of Della's dad, but it wouldn't have made any difference. He was what he was, and that's what he was, as Popeye would say.

Cynthia crying for Della, Della crying for Kierra, and who am I crying for? Everybody. It came on the news next morning—a small tornado ripped through this side of the mountain during the night, that was ME. And then a lot of rain, just rain.

Cynthia's cell phone rings around 5am, just as my rainstorm is starting to get serious, just as she's drifting to sleep, and of course it's Ted asking if she can come pick him up, and by the way it's only $2500 to release him into her care, which maybe she could loan him, and that's a good deal, a lucky thing, because he knows some of the people downtown, they shouldn't even let him out, not even for a million dollars. She stares at the phone a moment before hanging up on him. "This is why I live in Seattle," she tells the empty air. Then she hears Della's phone ringing, seven rings... Ted's trying to reach Della, but she's not answering. Then the front door creaking open—it's Tommy, finally, coming in from the rain—and then, silence, and then the murmur of Della's whisper, a small but very solid whisper, almost a swish, like a dam springing a leak.

Tommy replies, "It's your own damn fault, Della."

Time stops. I can hear his watch ticking.

○

Then louder voices, then a gush, like a rotten wind, then screaming—the dam that had held so long, that kept their determined but contrary relationship in place, has burst wide open, finally, just as the unsuspecting sun peeks up through my pretty poplar trees to start another day.

I don't know what to do except to guard her face from the flying objects—one minute he's kicking Kierra's toys across the room, then he's slumping against the wall, sobbing, it's a sort of worthless sobbing that Della has seen only one other time in their years together. He's sobbing because she swore to him that this time, she is leaving, and he saw it in her face that she meant it. He is sobbing like a little boy. Which means, take over, you are on your own here, Della.

So what if you are an orphan; he is a Bigger Orphan.

Fix this for me, he says. Fix this for everybody, Della.

That's what she gets for being a superwoman orphan, doing everything by herself all these years, or so she thinks, carrying anybody she meets piggy-back whether they ask her to or not. People notice this—especially a certain kind of person—they want you for themselves, you're always the one to listen to them, or to do for

them, and they come to expect that kind of service and they aren't
the kind of people to say thank you. I am talking about takers.
Takers are attracted to Della, just like takers were attracted to her
mother. They come along in a steady stream and use you up and
then act like they don't understand what's gone wrong, why you're
unhappy, or tired, or depressed. You're strong enough to do a lot
for people before you give up. You expect very little from others.
Not that you're perfect by any means, Della. You're only human!
And you've got this weak spot that looks like strength, but it isn't.
It's the reason you're in this situation and it's the reason you're going to have a hell of a time getting out of it.

Della will have to wait a full 48 hours to see her child, but
I'll be here for her, holding her in my heart the whole infinite time,
two days, a long drawn-out two days of nothing to draw on. Her
mother's available, awake in the guest room bed, but at the moment
I'm the better comfort.

O

Then Tommy's off to work, or off somewhere, which puts
an end to their quarrelling, and Della pulls herself together fairly
quickly after that. She eats most of the poached egg on toast pre-
pared by Cynthia, who serves it to her right there on the edge of the
sofa, her little safety perch. Della takes her time to eat, then she just
stares into space. Finally, when her watch beeps to let her know it's
time to leave the house for work, she's able to move. She puts
Kierra's toys back in place, dresses herself, throws water and makeup on her face. She'll be late by nearly a half hour. Cynthia
drives her to work and waits for a while, in case her daughter comes
running back out, but she doesn't and she won't.

Then Cynthia parks in a nearby parking lot where she gets
on the phone, to see about the case, to start working on whatever
she can do to help, and to check on Ted.

You might accuse me of being superwoman-orphan-ghost,
and that would be somewhat correct, but it's different. I'm not a
living mammal with offspring to raise. I can afford to dedicate myself to larger causes and many people. I won't lose energy or sleep
over it, because I don't use energy or sleep; to be honest, I'm not

sure what I run on. I do limit myself, though, to people I care for (chiefly, my descendents and the various living beings in their lives).

I did give it all I had to give, when I was living.

At this moment, just out of curiosity, I stay with Cynthia, my great-granddaughter, rather than following Della into work. I remain in the car, nestling next to Cynthia, listening in. She's on hold, and she's got the radio on at the same time, the morning news (how boring, same stories, different century). She taps the steering wheel in a peculiar rhythm that keeps company with her thoughts but has nothing to do with the news. Ah, I see, she's not listening to the news, she is not hearing a word of it. She's thinking about her brother. Ted. He was a baby once, her own twin brother. Somehow she's set aside her worries about her daughter's child, and her daughter's mental state, and she's not even watching what she seems to be looking at.

I've noticed that Cynthia knows her way around here, and suddenly, just now, that young look on her face, I remember she spent her teen years here, I remember that I looked in on some of that era. No, it was not just a dream; I looked in. Ted and Cynthia learned to drive here. Later on—up north—I tried to intervene when Cynthia went back to work full-time, Della still a little one, needing her. I took off, couldn't stand it, watching that precious Della coming up an orphan like me. I exaggerate—she had a lot more than I had growing up, but somehow it ended up feeling the same to her, BIG NEGLECT, and I do not like that even now, even though I haven't succeeded yet in stopping it from happening generation after generation after generation. It is my fault, you see, not yours Della. I've figured that's the main reason I am still here, trying to put it right. I vow to do so, this time, this generation. Enough is enough! I do have a feeling I have some help—from something bigger than me, like the culture, or something even less likely, not God exactly—maybe I'll get around to explaining my relationship with God later on—just something bigger that at first glance might look smaller. Something is helping me, this time around.

Sorry for being so unclear. It's an image forming in my mind's eye, though I have no material mind and no material eye, my entire being about as vague and fleeting and timeless as the fog on a bog before the day starts. I can almost see it, this helper of mine, and it moves on four legs, and it cries like Ted used to cry when he first came home from that war, a sort of a war cry, a determined sound. It's a scolding, hushing, insistent sound. It's bringing little Kierra back to us fast, running with her, moving in and out between the poplars, knocking snow from the hemlocks of my childhood, sledding down hillsides to get home to a place where fun finally happens. FUN!!

This being, this helper... It has something to do with Ted, very much, I see it in Cynthia's mind, a plan forming there that has nothing to do with the law and everything to do with Ted. She's kneading it between her fingers as she taps the steering wheel, drives a mile, turns left, drives another mile. She's taking her time getting to the jail, driving a bit out of her way, planning, plotting, and I think she's being used by some higher force, she's being driven to do something she herself doesn't even understand. I see dollar signs and with a start, followed by a nasty taste in my mouth, like I've bit my lip, I know she's planning to bail him out. This seems like a very very bad idea to me, considering how much that fellow can drink. It would do him good to dry out, and jail really helps support one's good intentions in that regard. Somebody has to take control. I'm glad I came along, my curiosity is intense, and I am not necessarily reassured when I see the intelligent gleam in Cynthia's eyes. I do not know what is stronger in her at this time in her life, her intelligence, or that gleam.

She's taking her time getting out of the car, partly because of her back, but mostly because she doesn't exactly want to be doing this. The very idea of bailing out her brother floods her little life with drama, much more drama than she wants—she's had her fill of that. Drama creates the gleam in her eye, but it also takes away any sparkle. It's mid-morning and the sun shines bright and steady on the crepe myrtle bushes that surround the city-county buildings, the kind of sheer straight light that makes the orangey-red myrtle blossoms glow, and turns the green shrubbery and ornamental grasses into something more like neon. A good day for a jail break, and that is exactly what she's doing, really, pulling out her checkbook before she even enters the building. She's going to write that check for her brother and haul him home, haul him somewhere, carry him all the way back to Seattle if necessary. She writes the check before she talks to him. In fact, she will not speak to him until he's fastened his seat belt.

"Ted," she says, as Ted steps into her red sub-compact rental car, moving his long skinny legs to one side to fit them in.

"I know," he answers, clicking his seat belt, and at the same time, putting his emotional shield up. His voice has that dutiful tone that makes Cynthia roll her eyes. "I messed up."

"You know more than I do about this family," says Cynthia, ignoring him, "and I'm tired of pretending that everything's okay, that everything's always been good."

"So... okay, go on," says Ted. "Let me have it."

"Yes indeed, there's a lot of good in this family or I guess we wouldn't be here, having this discussion."

"This car ride. This bailout, you mean." His eyes are trying to read her face.

"Well, blood's thick."

"And stickly, sis." He grins a rueful grin.

"Sticky," she corrects. "Yes, thick and sticky."

"Stickly. Prickly."

"Okay, anyway, I care about you Ted, even though you were way out of line, showing up at my daughter's house in that condition."

"Way off," Ted agrees, nodding.

"The social services people are going to go harder on her, because you were there. You know that."

"You think? I mean, I'm not the father or even the granddad. She don't have to tell them we're related even."

"Don't start. You were there, in her house. You went drunk driving from her house and you got picked up for the millionth time. Did she serve you alcohol? 'Cause that could get her in some more trouble."

"Let me think... I don't think she did. No. They don't drink much over there, do they? Tommy's always bumming a beer at our poker nights, I don't think she lets him buy it."

"You don't know? You mean you don't remember?"

"Heck no, Cindy, you know how it is, you black out sometimes, that's normal. You've blacked out when you drank, when you got drunk."

"No Ted, I haven't ever blacked out. I've never forgot what I said, where I went, what I did."

"Good for you then."

"Not good for me. That's not what I'm talking about. I'm saying, we need to get you out of town for a while. We need to take you up to the cottage and leave you there, and no whiskey to keep you company. We need you to be 'out of sight, out of mind,' especially with regard to Della, until this thing with her baby blows over."

"Ahh, sis, it don't matter. They don't care about me."

"I can put you right back in jail if I feel like it. I can rescind my pledge any time and they'll just pick you back up."

"You could but you wouldn't."

"Would."

"Wouldn't, couldn't."

"Shouldn't," Cynthia says, shooting an exasperated look at her brother.

"Okay go on then, let me have it. How long?"

"How long what?"

"How long you gonna trap me in that cabin."

"However long it takes."

"Can I bring the dog?"

"You have another dog?"

"I do, and she looks just like the puppy Della had, they could be out of the same litter, who knows."

"How do you afford a dog?"

He gives her a look.

"Seriously, Ted."

"Well... for one, I don't need no doctor for a dog, I don't believe in that, that's crazy. And two, what's good enough for me to eat, that's good enough for my dog. Except rabies, yes, I do get her a rabies shot. You bet."

"What kind of dog is it?"

"I don't know, she's a mutt. About 30 pounds of dog. After a lot of thought, I named her Jeff the Dog."

"Jeff. Good guard dog?"

"Jeff the Dog's her name. I wouldn't call her a guard dog, but she's a barky dog. She's a little dog, like Kierra's little dog. I got this one at the shelter. I think they might be related." He's leaning forward in his seat, all excited about it.

"Nice little dog?"

"You bet."

"Well then, yes, of course you can have your dog. Who's been watching the dog for you?"

"I let her run outside when I'm gone. She's got food and water, and if that runs out, she can go hunting."

Cynthia raises her eyebrows but says nothing.

"And my car. That's all I need, my dog and my car. Cindy, I know what you're thinking—"

"You don't need a car to get in trouble with, Ted. You don't have a driver's license, remember?"

"I know, I know, but Jeff the Dog, you see, she's used to sleeping in it. I'm not allowed to have a dog at my apartment, so she stays in the car at night. Don't worry! You can take the key. Just, let me follow you in my car this once, and don't worry I'm sober, they don't serve whiskey up at the jail. I know I don't have a license but I do this all the time, I swear it. I'll drive the car up there and park it. I'll follow you or you follow me, either way, I'll stick by you. I'll give you my word. I'll give you the key. Promise, promise, promise."

Cynthia's looking at him slanty-eyed. "Didn't they impound your car?"

Ted smiles. "They did."

"So what are we talking about here?"

"My other one. The old VW."

"Missy? You still have that? She passed inspection?"

Ted's blue eyes beam his answer, his cheeks flushing.

Cynthia sighs, giving it up. After all, it's not up to her to control the world. "Okay," she says. "But you give me the key."

"I will give YOU the key, sis."

And Ted WILL give Cynthia the key just as he said he would, and of course he also has a spare one in the glove box that he does not tell his sister about, she doesn't need to know, she doesn't want to know, and that's why she doesn't think to ask about such things. Besides, she's got her mind on Della.

Cynthia's growing on me. She's grown up a lot, since I last looked in on her and she was struggling to raise Della on her own, shuffling that poor child back and forth in that crazy shared custody arrangement that Della's father insisted on. Of course when his car got repossessed she did all the driving and why she did it I do not understand, but that's all over now, long over, because he disappeared from the picture when Della was 12 or so, and I am not clear whether he died or just took off. That's 20 years ago. If he's alive, he doesn't know he has a little grandchild with leukemia, taken away from her family because of a river otter (who might have done it on purpose).

TEN

I'd better go check on my littlest girl. I know the address, since I can wisp my way into that cast-iron social services building (it's got its cracks) and read whatever papers they've got laying out here and there on their desks. My little grand-grand-girl Kierra, she's in a small, three-bedroom brick ranch house out Highway 74, off of Garrens Gap. She's been placed with a couple of Buddhists who've spent their lives taking in foster babies, not being able to have kids of their own. I read all that, more or less, in the papers on Mr. Pearson's desk. That's basically what they said, anyway; you can't exactly spell out people's private business, like not being able to have kids, unless they are a client and then every detail goes into the file, including misinformation and hearsay.

I leave Cynthia and Ted when they arrive at Ted's apartment on their mission to pick up the dog, a toothbrush, and Ted's car. I'm tickling them both across the shoulders as if to say, "I'll be back." I wouldn't want them to think I didn't care about them as much as I do about the others, but they ignore me of course, as if I don't exist. I am used to that. I'm hovering, hesitating, wishing they would at least wave, looking down on them as they get out of the car in unison, both of them holding their lower backs and limping a bit, which makes me wonder if they're lopsided like me— maybe it runs in the family. They're twins, and the older they get the more alike they look, both of them with their bushy eyebrows, wiry grey hairs mixed in with the original black hair. His is curly, hers is straight. His hair's going white in the front, while she's got two streaks one on each side above the ears. She's got two piercings in each ear and a flower tattoo on her left shoulder in honor of her most recent boyfriend, the one who died last fall (the one she never told Della about). Ted stumbles on his own front steps, and suddenly Cynthia's got her brother by the elbow, making sure he keeps moving forward. That's sometimes the hardest thing for people: moving forward, not sideways or back or in circles.

They push forth into the apartment lobby and Ted presses floor 6 as if he's on automatic now. All he needed was that little push. He'll need no further prodding, until it is time to turn around (having collected his toothbrush)—time to find his dog and his car, go on down that long road to hide out and dry up.

So that's where I leave them. I'm flying across sparkling clouds, the air so thin and cold up here you can't breathe it, but I don't need to breathe so it's all good. I don't have to hold my breath in order to preserve it, and I don't need to slow down my breath in order to relax, I don't depend on anything like that, I'm telling you it's a wonderful freedom being body-less. My wisps blend in with the clouds, my fingers are like thin feathers, my shoulders are soft wings. I feel both embraced and at one with the clouds as I descend through them, embraced, yes, and chilled, loved, nourished. I've gone from an 80% water-filled body to 100% water, that's what my ghostly wisps are made of: unpolluted, clear, invisible water. I can create rainbows if the sun hits me just so, and that's what I'll do for my little Kierra when I first see that child, I will become a rainbow for her. She'll feel my presence because she is still young enough to see people like me, still young enough to see with eyes other than the two fleshy ones that require constant fresh blood in order to work, which in turn requires food and clothing and water and warmth. It's really quite an enterprise, staying in the body, holding onto that God-given contraption. No wonder it requires such a will to live, if you give up even a little bit it's not far to go, to be gone from that particular existence, as dense as it might feel at the time.

I'm here. It's just like the picture on Mr. Pearson's desk. The front yard has been dug up, I mean, no grass—just a flower and vegetable garden, a collection of artsy-looking rocks balanced one upon the other, and then, off to the side, there really is a line of bowling balls making a border between their garden and the neighbors' grass yard. I thought I saw bowling balls in the photograph. Sure enough. Their walkway is made out of broken shards of tile, brightly colored, mismatched. And now there's a rainbow coming up that walkway and it's me, and in less than an instant I am through the screen door (screens being porous), and I run smack into a plethora of rainbows—looks like a roomful of cousins of mine, but it's an illusion. Sun catchers, that's all. These people have sun catchers across all the front windows, large and tiny and medium-sized prisms hanging on see-through fish line, making so many rainbows that I'm a little embarrassed at first, that being my main skill when it comes to children. You can see that mine is the biggest rainbow, but I'm outnumbered. No matter. There's Kierra, asleep on the sofa, her skinny arm flung up across a stuffed panda bear, an old looking cat—a real one, long haired and calico—pressed up against her pink little feet, no socks, no shoes. Her diaper smells clean, and her face is freshly washed, and she looks peaceful enough in her sleep. To the left, just inside the kitchen, there's a middle-aged woman standing on a rag rug doing dishes by hand, listening to NPR, and at the same time humming some tune that I never heard before—it could be a Buddhist song I suppose. I'm always interested in learning, so I'm listening hard, but I can't make it out, and I can't find a place in her mind where she's stored the words to that song that she's humming. I like the tune, though. I know nothing about Buddhism, except that it is not a type of a Baptist.

There's some kind of soup on the stove and it lacks meat, I can tell that much with one whiff of it, even without a nose. Don't ask me to explain.

There are more sun catchers in the window over the kitchen sink, I think they are overdoing it a little. And above the kitchen table I see three bright, acrylic, abstract paintings of a rocky hillside with trees up above it, paintings that are made on pieces of wood, unframed, three versions of the same view. Those paintings stop me in my tracks, if I made tracks. I hover above the table studying them, smiling in my soul-heart because this place looks just like my rock, three paintings from three different angles, my own rock, the original rock where everything stopped more than a century ago. I swear it's my rock. All at once I have this uncanny feeling that I am home, these are my people. You can't blame me that I would linger and look.

O

After a while I'm floating around some more, moving on, skimming across the linoleum, tossing the dust-bunnies out of my way, and I notice that the nice lady's ankles are swollen. She's wearing house slippers shaped like bumblebees, but you can still see that her ankles are swollen. Not only that, the lady is wearing a turban that covers up all of her hair. Yes, it's a turban all right. Maybe they're Muslims. No, I can see her freckled neck and she's got some pretty, flashy earrings dangling down from her ears underneath that turban, and flashes of yellow hair, so she's not a Muslim, at least, not a fundamentalist one. She's not modest enough to be any sort of a fundamentalist, even a Buddhist fundamentalist, however that might look. I guess she's an artist, that would explain it.

Now she's drying her hands on a kitchen towel; then, even though her hands are dry she wipes them against her slacks, then she's scratching her nose, then reaching for the radio on top of the refrigerator to turn it down. She's just a little fidgety, I don't know why. She half-closes the kitchen door behind her as she approaches little Kierra. She sits down on the sofa pushing the long-haired cat to make room, and clasps one of Kierra's feet in her hand, and then... she just sits. For a moment, she's interchangeable with my Della—same slumped posture, same silence, same foot holding. She's a mother, all right. It's as if Kierra has willed it, to comfort herself. Somehow she made sure she got a good foster home, if that can even be done. The radio's playing classical music now, I barely hear the sound of it coming out of the kitchen, because of the door, and because the lady's thoughts are noisy. I read a thought: She is playing the radio for the baby, because sound is comforting, or, she hopes so, but sometimes she wonders what to do. Sometimes she wonders if there is anything she can do, after all these years of fostering babies, she feels less and less sure of things. Less and less sure of everything. Music? Soothing? I didn't know that, but you see, I am still learning. When I was a baby we didn't listen to radios—no—we listened to birdsong and creeks and wind, and each other. There were songs and drums and whistles and flutes, and the occasional horn sound. It makes sense, as I watch them now, the lady holding Kierra's little foot, humming now and then: it makes all the sense in the world to surround a little being with a bit of friendly noise, to help soothe them when they wake up, realizing with a start that they are not where they are supposed to

be. But I agree, I'm not sure the radio's the ticket. It's not real.
We didn't have such things when I was so young like that, but there
was always the creek, singing to me personally. I would have to say,
all in all, that I still prefer my creek, but this is nice too, so why not.
Also, why not have music for babies who are not in foster care?
For babies in the nursery daycare at church, and for babies whose
mothers stay home with them.

Kierra sleeps on and on, as if drugged. She sleeps as if she
is drinking in sleep, as if she were parched, an endless sleep recepta-
cle, nothing more and nothing less than an empty vessel that lives
for sleep. I understand this. She's drugging herself the only way
she can. Everything has stopped for her. There is no movement,
no action here. Nothing to run to or run from. It looks to me like
these people really know what they are doing, they have an understanding about this foster work they do, and my guess is they do it
well. Kierra will be okay here. I can feel it. There are no sinister
vibes in the back corner, no garbage bin or woodshed full of empty
bottles back behind the house, no dog or goat on a chain living in a
circle of dirt. The cat's happy, and the lady sits still and silent and
patient until her head tilts back and she sleeps, still holding Kierra's
foot. Even so, Kierra knows everything has stopped and that no
one can promise her life will ever be the same, once everything
starts going again.

I've seen the foster lady, but not the foster man. I'll wait
around, see what the man looks like. I wait and wait and wait, until
it's time for Della to come off work and he still hasn't shown up
yet, and I've got to get back to Della, I've just got to, so I give up
for now. I put a blessing on the snoozing lady and my sleeping
beauty Kierra. I thank Mrs. Foster Care Person again and again,
thanking her for watching out for Kierra so kindly, thanking her on
behalf of Della and Cynthia and myself of course, and I'm off
through the sky, giving myself a little push from the red tin roof of
the Buddhists' cottage. I swear I know these people, but from
where? It's been more than fifty years since I died and a lot of people look a lot alike, that's a fact, even though fashions change. If I
think long and hard enough I might come up with an answer,
though. I might figure out where that sweet lady comes from, de-
scends from. I haven't seen Mr. Foster Care Person yet, but I saw

his photo on Pearson's desk, and that man looked so familiar, he could be a brother if I ever had one.

But wait.

Wait. Speaking of brothers. There's only one car in the world with a purple peace sign painted on the roof so that you can see it from my vantage point. He's heading up the road, heading in the direction I just came from, winding steadily along Rose Road, taking a back way but nevertheless I can see where he's headed. Ted's on the move. Another U-turn for me.

Sure enough, he's pulling over, pulling into an empty lot a quarter mile from the foster parents, and he's cut the engine, and he's stepping out, not one bit drunk, I can see that. His face looks soft, but determined. He's walking like an Indian scout, and by now there probably is some of that native blood in us; it could come two ways—from the high north, or from those Hanafords (a lot of the Negroes had some Indian blood) and my oh my the way he tiptoes through the woods, he's so quiet he's almost a ghost like me and I'm almost proud of him, if it weren't for the fact that I need to concentrate right now. The problem is, I cannot read his thoughts. He's blanking out on me. A blank mind and a moving body?—that's never a good combination, no good will come of it. I'm weaving about, stirring up the wind, circling him, trying to make him cold so that he goes back to his car for his jacket, then maybe I can rig the door somehow, trap him in the car. But no, he just shivers and keeps on, stubborn man. He is stone sober and I am not sure if I like that—he's less predictable in this condition.

He knows he can't run, or he'd make noise. He just keeps walking, steady, determined. He doesn't want to turn back now, for some reason that doesn't make any sense to me. But then I see it: a stray picture-poem wanders out from the top of his scalp and comes to me like a lost dog, lands in my hands. It's a picture of Mr. Foster Person. Ted knows the man. He knows where he lives, he knows Kierra is here and he knows the man won't be home for another hour. All that spills out in pictures, not words.

He wants to get over there before the man gets home. For what? At times like this, I wish I had someone to consult, something besides the empty wind, the smooth talking water, the dandruffy animals and snoopy spiders. They don't get it. They think this is ridiculous stuff, this human tribulation, that this is none of their concern …but I want to tell them it IS THEIR CONCERN because don't you know WE ARE ALL CONNECTED! Seeing as humans don't listen to the trees, maybe it is up to the trees to listen to the humans. C'mon now. Listen up.

This line of thought seems to get his attention: Ted seems to hear me because he stops. He's thinking it over. I get another vision: he knows the foster man as a friend, an old friend. No… not a friend. A teacher. Yes, I see it! And Ted nods a confirmation to me—that he sees me, too. I feel it, his awareness, and it makes me feel warm all over. I can't see myself in a mirror but I imagine I'm blushing with happiness.

It comes to me full on, the memory of a meditation class falls on top of me so that I have to sit down and simply be in it, along with Ted. We're remembering together—I love this! Ted's slumping, then sitting on his heels. He's counting his breaths. Ted? Sitting still? Breathing? Maybe he'll turn around—I mean that literally, maybe he'll turn around and go on home, right now. That would be best. But for now, I'm sitting in class with him, watching the teacher's mouth as he says to breathe, just so, without worrying whether it is just so or not just so. The teacher's mouth is soft and kind and that seems to have an effect on Ted's mouth. The teacher's face is almond brown. The teacher's chest is large with space where once there was violence. Yes, violence. This teacher is a war vet of some sort? Maybe. But right now, he's just sitting, breathing, one man in a circle of other veterans, saying nothing, no teaching, no preaching. In the place of big violence there is big silence. Ted's standing up again, and at first I don't even know it, because I am still watching the teacher's wrinkled face, he seems to be aging as he teaches, which tells me it has been years since Ted sat with him. His name is coming to me… Mr. Foster Person has a name. Lawrence. Yes. Lawrence Something. I am breathing, resting, while Ted creeps away from me—this is how he gave me the slip, I will never forget it. He saw me, without my knowing it, and gave me a vision that would stop me in my tracks, so that he could slip away, go about his business. He is in touch with my world more than I knew, and he, like Lawrence, has some great space within him, a boundlessness that he plans to use, now, in this lifetime, for one particular purpose. He's not going to let me stop him.

Next thing I know he's at their front door, ringing the bell, setting their dog to barking, startling the cat, waking Kierra, and I'm still drifting about in the woods. I rush to catch up—Ted alone feels my arrival.

Kierra comes to the door with her keeper, pretty much glued to the lady's hip, and since she has so few memories of Ted and has been slung about so much from one stranger to the next in the past 24 hours, she shows no sign of recognition or friendship.

"Hello?" the lady says.

"Hi, you must be Maggie? I'm an old student looking for Mr. Castleman. He taught meditation at the Light Center back in the 90's."

"Of course! Yes, I'm Maggie. We met one time. You're Ted."

"That's right. I'm sorry, I don't remember things all that well, but now that you mention it… your face is familiar. Yes. Well. I don't know if Mr. Castleman will remember me, but I appreciate that you do. Thank you. Is that your baby?"

"Yes, she's ours for the moment, we're fostering. This is Kierra."

Kierra shakes her head no. She's wiping her hands together like there is something on them, a nervous little gesture that Maggie often sees in her foster children when they first arrive. Kierra does not want to be hugged or touched or held by anyone other than Maggie, because, as far as she can tell, she's safe with Maggie. She does not want to move, there's been enough of that. She recognizes Uncle Ted, but you wouldn't know it from the look on her face.

Ted ignores the child, which is a good idea on his part. "Well, how can I get in touch with Mr. Castleman?"

"Call back in about an hour. He's teaching right now, but he'll be home soon. I know! Why don't you leave him your phone number. Then I can have him give you a call, first chance he gets, okay?"

Ted's already writing out his number on the back of a Walmart receipt. "Thanks," he says, thrusting it into her free hand. "Tell him I really appreciate it. And I appreciate the work he's doing with the veterans, if he's still doing that. I quit drinking because of him," he adds, because he always has to add a little something extra, a little something more, a small lie, like a punctuation mark at the end of the sentence. The truth is, he did stop drinking and he remained sober for two weeks after leaving the meditation class. "It helps, helps a lot."

"He IS still doing it, yes." A generous smile. "I'll tell him. He can always use a positive word."

"Thanks."

Ted turns to go. He looks back once, casting his eyes, then his soul, over his shoulder, but Maggie's gone. I fly out ahead of him, nervous, for no reason—no one can see me, other than Ted. Ted's walking back up the road to the car. Soon he's stomping along like a man on a mission, like he's suddenly determined something inside of his mind. I'm a few yards ahead now, watching him coming, stomping up the hill like an old bull, and he passes right through me, on purpose, a quarrelsome son, then continues on down through the trees to his little hidden parking spot. He climbs into his rusting car, just sits down behind the wheel and stares out the dirty windshield, massaging his lower back. He's waiting for me to catch up. He's offering me a ride, in fact, I know it. I'm curious enough to take it, and when I've settled myself somewhere between the passenger seat and the rear view mirror, he starts the engine. Well. It turns out the family cabin is only 15 minutes from here, up near Gerton off of Bear Wallow Road. Out here in mountain country, that's like being next-door neighbors. When Ted drives the car up across the yard to the front steps and parks it there in the grass, Jeff the Dog greets us from inside the house with a volley of barks like bullets that you can hear all across the valley, even down there at Kierra's foster home. Jeff's a fierce little mutt, white with yellow patches, short hair, snarly mouth, wagging tail, her nose pressed up against the glass of the living room window. I'd say she's a pretty little thing, and well-trained, it turns out. She'll sit on a dime, even with me flying about her, trying to pet her in my own way. Dogs have always liked me, and now's no exception. Jeff's spindly white tail is going so fast it might come right off. Ted sees it, and smiles directly at me as if he sees ME.

"You like it in the house, don't you girl?" he says, sympathetically. He opens the door to let her run out and pee. While she's outside he mixes up a bowl of the kibble Cynthia bought, mixes it with some of the leftover Chinese food he brought from his apartment, then whistles her back in. He leaves her gobbling her meal in the back kitchen, steps out of the house to sit on the front stoop. He's staring off into the distance in the direction of the valley where his little grand-niece is holed up with the Buddhists. I can see he's contemplating, no—he's obsessing—and in between his mental sentences I can see that he's open to my advice if I can work it in somehow, between his rapid thoughts—there is the slightest crack. Suddenly, we're in this together. He's actually giving it some genuine thought: is Kierra better off with those infernal Buddhist-type people, or should he get her out of there? If she's got cancer (Cynthia told him), then does she not deserve to live out her little life in peace, with her own mother? Should someone not save Kierra from this abandonment to some stand-in with swelled ankles and a turban, who does not smell, walk or talk like her real mother? But Lawrence, that's another matter, Ted knows something about that man. Ted couldn't catch on to meditating, but there was something about Lawrence that stuck with him all these years, something brotherly about him, something motherly, even in the eyes.

The enduring problem with Ted is that he's too bright for this world, and because of that, he turned off his compassion when he saw too much and did too much when he was much too young to be killing people. When he turned off the compassion, most of his intuition went out the window too. So it's hard for him to think things through, in spite of his vast intelligence. It's as if the brains and the guts are no longer connected, the wires severed permanently when the thing happened with the little girl.

He's blank again, I can't read it. He's not drinking, not yet—Cynthia made sure he didn't smuggle any alcohol into the cabin, and so far he's resisted the beer he found already there—right there in the fridge, four cans in the side of the door. But the problem is, a seething depression waits right outside the front door of his spirit trapping him inside his own self, keeping him from going anywhere. It's been either drink or despair ever since he returned from Viet Nam, and he's mostly chosen to drink, because at least he can find a few friends to keep him company when he's drinking, happy people who know how to have a little fun along the way, people who don't expect anything. It's a sort of ironic fun that they have.

But now Ted has a third choice appearing somewhere on the perimeter, a vague presence of something, an opening, a way out. It has to do with his old teacher, and with Kierra, and with me. I know it through and through: Somehow the three of us—Lawrence, Ted, and me—will free little Kierra and keep her safe as well. Ted knows it too, in the same way that a person knows his own name. His intuition is not completely dead. He's got an understanding that connects him up with me, and it warms my spirit. We'll do something about Kierra all right. The question is what to do and how to go about it. You can thrash around a lot in life, thinking you are changing things when really you are just making them worse, or recasting them so they look different when deep down they are not any different at all. For example, throwing away your Bible for a self-help book. Trading your therapist for a minister or vice-versa. Separating from your parents and then remarrying them in the person you choose for a partner. Promising you'll not harm your kids the way you were harmed, so you harm them some other way that ends up feeling the same to them, if not worse. What I'm saying is: For Ted to pull this off, he'll have to stop drinking so much, and is that possible. I mean: What will take its place?

ELEVEN

He's got a beer open now (it didn't take long, did it?), but he's barely touched it. "Don't move too fast," I tell him, and he's actually listening. "Watch what you do, no sudden moves," I say, and he knows what I mean, because he freezes right where he is, and he nods in agreement, as if he's actually listening, as if he understands my point. I've got myself across his shoulders like a good wool shawl, cuddling him, poor shivering thing. He's already got the evening jitters and pretty soon he'll be sipping that beer, then gulping it, so I pour it on while I have the chance. I shout, "Ted, this is your great-grandmother talking to you!"

He's completely receptive. "Hey, Granny. I don't believe we've met."

"Close your eyes, and see if you can see me."

"With my eyes closed?" He downs the rest of the beer in three strong glugs, reaches for another can.

"Yes, your eyes closed, and hold off on that second beer for a minute."

"Yes Ma'am." He's got them closed. His hand clasps and unclasps the second beer in rhythm with his pulse.

"You're going to have to stop drinking."

He slumps his shoulders in response.

"Just for a few days, son, do you think you can do that?"

"No, not really."

"For your granny?"

"We never really met, Grandma. But I'd like to see you happy. I don't begrudge people their happiness."

"Then put the beer down, Ted, and listen."

He sighs, sets it down. He stands up, walks over to the television, picks up the remote. Next thing I know he's got a show on, the latest thing, something called Gleam or Glee or something like that. He's not going to listen. Not now. I don't like television but it's better than beer I suppose. He's determined to tune me out; he's putting a hand up against his temple and pressing hard, trying to fend off the migraine and yet welcoming it, in a way. If the migraine comes we won't be able to talk again for three days. I'm giving him some kind of grief, which I don't understand, but I know it's me stirring something up for him, something too difficult, so I fly up, up and way out through the dark night, to give him some peace. I'm gone, but I've got with me a shard of information, I'm carrying something off with me, something of his, a memory he doesn't want, a dark-skinned baby girl who wanted to live, that's all she wanted, to live, that's what she said to him as her spirit slipped away like a salamander into a tiny crevice in a rock wall, she slipped out of anyone's reach. As she left, he heard it in perfect English even though that was not her language, she spoke to him in the in-between ethers, the place where they could see each other clearly. She wanted to live, even without her leg, she wanted to keep living. The memory sparkles in my hand like a piece of polished agate. I will keep it for him—that's what he's asking, in return for his help.

And in the morning, sure enough, he wakes up sober. He didn't drink that second beer, and though he has a headache coming on, he has a mission, stronger than ever, I can tell by the way he's stomping around the cabin. He knows he can hold out sober at least a week, but migraines come and go on their own schedule. He's got to hold out on all of it: the alcohol and the migraine and the jitters and whatever else might sneak up on him from behind, but his main concern is the migraine and the alcohol. If he's lucky, he'll have a few days of clarity before one or the other comes on, either the drink or the headache, or both, and he knows that's not much time, those demons hounding him already, nipping at his heels, blinding him from himself and everything else that matters, so we'll have to move fast.

Around 7am, Lawrence Castleman calls Ted up. His calm, sincere voice is unchanged from years ago, and yes he's still leading a meditation for veterans, and he's missed seeing Ted all these years. He's quite earnest about it. He remembers Ted because of that spiritual piece so apparent in the man, it showed like a red scarf around his throat, bright, worn, ripped, but still in place, still intact, and Ted's bright heart—it shone out through his eyes, once or twice, unmistakable to someone like Lawrence, practiced in mindful observing, mindful listening. Ted never could close his eyes during meditation, and he could never bring himself to face the wall, and eventually he quit because of those two things, or so he said. Lawrence smiles as he talks and Ted can hear the smile in his old teacher's voice. It's time to go back for a visit, and though it seems he's being sidetracked already, I think this is a good thing.

"Go," I whisper, "He holds the class in his own living room. You'll get to see Kierra and we'll know what to do."

"When do you meet?" Ted asks.

"Thursdays at 6pm, and Tuesdays at 6am." As usual, Lawrence doesn't press Ted to come, to convert, to change anything at all.

"I'm coming," Ted replies.

"That would be wonderful," Lawrence smiles through the phone, "it'll be great to see you again." He hangs up with no expectation that he'll ever see Ted again, but he's smiling, savoring the connection, breathing in the memory of Ted's bright eyes almost closing, how close Ted came to touching peace, almost—almost—shuttering the intelligence and the paranoia (so intertwined as to be one thing)—how close, for one moment, he came to True Self, the vast "I am." Scared the hell out of him. On his trek toward peace, Ted touched something hot, like the rage of ten million men, the hot lid on the pot on the stove. So he quit. Wouldn't you do the same?

As soon as Ted hangs up, I give him a big push out of the house (he has got to keep moving). When his door slams, I'm over to Lawrence's. In the blink of a salamander's eye, I will it, I wish it, I swish my tail once and I'm there in "no time." Ha!

O

Lawrence breathes out, one long solid breath, and turns to Maggie who has just entered the room, Kierra on her hip. "That was Ted," he says, but Maggie already knows.

Lawrence is an unusual fellow. I'm studying him right now at this moment, because I see how important he is to Ted. I want a closer look. Obviously he claims some indigenous ancestry; from the photographs in the hallway I see a blurry maternal great-grandmother of some generations back, small and dark, her tiny slits of eyes squinting into the sun, and all that's left now in Lawrence is a faint olive cast to his skin, and that Asian fold over the eye. He's short and lean like his European Jewish ancestors, and his curly hair makes one wonder if he's part black, which he is not. He's greying now, with more width about the waist, but the old panic and anxiety that plagued him in his youth is tamed from decades of meditation. He never went to war, because he was able to get off on a psychiatric condition, those same panic attacks, diagnosed and embellished by Uncle Marty's friend Lew, who happened to be Lawrence's godfather, but nobody needed to know that.

Maggie says, "He's coming back?"

Lawrence shakes his head. "Maybe, we'll see. I hope so." But he knows that pretty much, when Maggie says something like that, she's right—it wasn't really a question, it was a statement. "I'd like to see him again," Lawrence adds, reaching out for Kierra.

Kierra sees and smells safety here, though it is all different and she does not like that. There is no sound of arguing, no smell of pancakes burning in the skillet while Mommy dries her hair with that handheld hair dryer that always shuts off before her hair is dry, and then the sound of whiney grumbling, and Tommy taking over, throwing the burnt pancakes off the deck for the chipmunks and raccoons. They don't have real milk here—instead it is something watery and sweet (rice milk)—and they try to make her eat oatmeal. She stares at Lawrence, evaluating him. He looks very strange to her, and he smells so different from her daddy, and this strange man looks at her like he sees her, which she loves but at the same time it overwhelms and frightens her. He's smiling, then turning away, without pressing her to come to him, and now she's riding Maggie's hip into the kitchen where French toast sizzles in a pool of olive oil, smelling of cinnamon, smelling wonderful. She takes an interest in this, although in her heart something feels empty, wrong, like she's going to die. There's the first inkling of guilt, that she would enjoy someone else's mothering, someone else's home, that she might want this home, but she also wants her old home back. She screws her little mouth up as if to cry, but her hunger overrides her fear, and she reaches, without meaning to, reaches out for the food.

"Hot," says Maggie.

"Hot," Kierra replies, recoiling dutifully.

"Ooh, you said that very good," Maggie says. "You can talk!"

"Hot," Kierra says again, swelling to the praise.

And she likes her new high chair which is all clean and shiny white. She likes the French toast, sliced into tiny squares. She eats it all up, every last bite. She throws her fork on the floor, looks up at Maggie: nothing happens. She likes the rainbows painted all over the kitchen walls—by a rising sun shining through the crystals hanging in the window above the sink—and she likes it when Maggie notices, and she likes the crystal that Maggie places in her little hand. She likes Maggie's soft voice, and when she puts her hand up to feel Maggie's face, she likes the soft and fluffy cheeks of her new caregiver. In this moment she is not upset at all. She's on a new path, she's entering a new life that invites her to feel happy, and that happiness tastes like food in her mouth, like warm milk.

When Lawrence walks by, she just watches him. Her belly is full, and she knows she is safe here.

He goes out the back door, letting it bang shut behind him, then in a flash he's coming back in. In, and out. Out, and in. He's feeding a dog out back, first a bowl of chow, then a fresh bowl of water. She can barely see a blur of yellow fur, a swishing tail, gratitude. Kierra points in that general direction, and Maggie says, "Dog. His name is Thaddeus. You met him yesterday, in the house, remember? Thaddeus."

Then Lawrence is back inside, sits down next to Kierra, and Maggie sets a plate of breakfast in front of him. He's not eating that sweet French toast. Instead he has something that looks like hay, some kind of wheat cereal, and on top of that a mound of bran, and on top of that, rice milk, because he is vegan. Vegan? Just when I think I've learned everything.

I'm swimming around above the table blending in with the steam from the teapot, which has come to a boil, and I'm breathing in the hot moist air and the quiet calm. I want to stay here too, I want to be adopted into this strange little family, this small, tidy house so quiet you could hear a pin drop, except for the dog which has just now decided to set himself to barking at something. That's a frantic bark. Then the sound of scrambling canine paws careering around the house to the front yard, climbing the porch—

toenails clattering against wood—then standing ground, barking. Someone's here.

I float up to the clock and stare into its face: 8am, a beautiful sunny beginning of a day. I am not really surprised that Ted has followed my instructions, but at the same time, I AM surprised. I can't get over that people are finally hearing me, first Della, now Ted. And in Ted's case, not only hearing me, but following my directions. Ted's here to look in on Kierra, make sure she's okay, and he knows better than to admit any connection to the child. Our plan is not fully formed. We're still gauging the situation, scoping things out. We are a team. I almost feel alive, linked arm in arm with Ted on a soul-saving mission.

Thaddeus stops barking because Ted allows him to sniff him up, and the dog is sitting calmly next to Ted by the time Lawrence opens the front door.

"Ted?" he says. Of course it's Ted.

"Hi Larry. I thought I'd come by for the meditation, but I don't see any other cars, am I too early?"

"Well..." Lawrence replies, "actually... this is the wrong day, and the wrong time, theoretically." Then, something seems to come over him—it's me, actually, nudging him in the ribs—and he smiles. "But seeing as you're here, it must be the right day and the right time."

"I thought you said Tuesdays at 6am?"

"I did. This is Thursday, though, and it is closer to 8."

Ted's embarrassed. I pushed him out the door, lying to him about the time just to get him out of the house, to get things rolling. I had the strong intuition that Lawrence would receive him, and we really couldn't wait. With this kind of situation you can't lose momentum. People in Ted's shoes get stuck so easily, they can go around in circles for years until they forget what they started out to do. It's like a reverse spiral, like a whirlpool in Laurel Creek. You really have to get behind their shoulder blades and push. Put your ghostly hands behind those kidneys and push. Yank on them if they're caught on something, then push some more. Push. You don't have to push hard, just keep pushing. He wants to go back to his whiskey, his favorite method of treading water, swimming in circles. He had such a tendency from birth, but then the 'Nam experience nailed it into him, this particular type of slow motion. He really just can't move forward much, when it comes to the functions of normal everyday life. "Normal" doesn't make a lot of sense to him, which I understand. There's a lot of busywork to it, not nearly enough laziness and artistry, not on this continent.

"I'll come back on Tuesday, then," he says.

"Sure. Or you can come on in, I was about to sit. Join me, if you like."

Ted nods, thinking it over. He'd rather leave, but his old teacher seems sincere, and that's correct, he is. He is also more relaxed. A few years ago he never would have invited a student into his house so informally. Maybe he's more confident about himself after all these years of teaching, and part of it is that Lawrence understands about Ted, that Tuesday could roll around and the whole thing would be forgotten by then. At the VA they call it PTSD or Attention Deficit, but Lawrence doesn't see it that way. If that's what Ted has, then we all have it, it's the water we swim in, according to Lawrence.

He doesn't know why Ted would come knocking on his door just now, but he doesn't particularly need to know. He sees an opportunity for a fraction-of-an-inch more peace in the world. He sees that Ted might be ready for some help, but not well enough to tell time. Not that that's Lawrence's problem. The best way I can put it is that just by sticking around, Lawrence has gotten to a place in life where he just cares about people, without needing to explain it, and to a place where he does not care so much about time. For the most part, he leaves it at that rather than trying to explain himself. (Maggie says he's becoming "old fashioned," caring about the neighbors like his grandpa taught him.) Whatever the reason, who cares, he'd just like to see Ted sitting every day, finding that quiet peace, just because he would enjoy that, because he cares about it, that big quiet place some people sometimes find by sitting and breathing into it, by listening, by getting still inside and out. Somehow it's easy for me to get a read on this man; it's like it's just not so murky in there as you usually would find.

"Really, it's no trouble for me, if you'd like to stay."

Maggie comes up behind him, Kierra locked onto her hip; Kierra registers some recognition of Ted but she doesn't lean toward him, nor does she recoil. It's imperceptible, their connection, the middle-aged alcoholic white man and the tan, curly haired babe.

For all his years of meditation and mindfulness practice, Lawrence doesn't pick up on this connection. Maggie, having that motherly instinct, can feel the shift in Kierra's body but she doesn't know how to name it. She assumes Kierra is a little uncomfortable with a new person coming into the house.

As if she knows what Maggie is wondering, Kierra says, "Ta-ta," in an effort to speak Ted's name. But she maintains her grip on her caregiver.

"Ta ta?" Maggie asks.

But Kierra is silent; she clings to Maggie like a little bird, her rosy cheeks puffed out as if she could spew out an entire sentence, a whole paragraph of explanation.

"Ta ta," Maggie repeats, kindly, softly, as if she understands, and Ted smiles suddenly, a burst of light coming through his eyes, sun behind clouds, and Kierra dances on Maggie's hip, a happy little jig.

He can't risk anything. He's grey again, grey and silent and unsmiling.

○

TWELVE

"Come in, then," Lawrence says. Ted forces a little smile at Maggie and Kierra, a polite smile that won't elicit a response from the baby, as he follows Lawrence into a small, second living room that has been swept of almost all furniture, almost all dust. There's a solitary mat with a pillow on it, obviously Lawrence's spot, close to the window. Behind that, a stack of mats and a stack of pillows. In a neat row on a narrow bench below the windowsill, a small bowl of sand, a cup of clear water, a single flower and a bell. A box of incense and a book of matches.

"Do you remember much about meditation?" Lawrence asks, picking out a stick of incense.

Ted shrugs. "I probably do. It'll come back to me."

"Would you like some instruction?"

"No. No, I'll figure it out. We'll see how well I can remember."

He watches while Lawrence puts his palms together and makes a little bow, lights the incense, another bow. Silence. Then Lawrence picks up the bell and sits on his pillow, rings the bell, a sweet sound that makes little ringing waves through the room and out the door. It almost hurts Ted's head, it kind of needles him. More silence. Ted stands for a moment, watching, then realizes it is time to sit. He takes a mat and a pillow and places them like Ted's, sits, squirms, crosses and uncrosses his legs. He can't quite bend the left knee, that's the one he permanently injured during basic training while "running off" a sprain, but he finally finds a sort of peace in his posture. He can't remember how to do this, really. The minutes tick by—it is so quiet, he can hear Lawrence's watch— and I am dancing about the two of them, encouraging Ted, breathing with Lawrence, but I can't sit still any better than Ted can. I begin whispering at him, arranging our plans, still giddy that he can hear me.

"We could take Kierra, but that would only make it worse for Della," I'm saying, and Ted thinking it right along with me. "Plus, the little girl doesn't trust you, Kierra's seen you drunk and she knows you have a problem with her.... you do, don't you. You're afraid. What is it?"

In the silence, he sees Kierra's plump brown body toddling, her first steps, which she inadvertently took towards Ted a year and two months ago, and everyone cried out, "she's walking," which scared her and made her cry. That was the last time he went over there until Cynthia arrived last week. It strikes him, all at once, in this maddening silence, that Kierra looks Vietnamese, she just hints at it, but it's there, and then he's staring at the back of Lawrence's neck, noting that Lawrence also has some Asian streak in him, whether it's Native American, Philippine, or Sami or Inuit, who knows, who cares. Something about him, but his name... Castleman... that's Jewish? Ted wants a drink. The urge is stirring up from his solar plexus grabbing at his neck, begging, demanding, pulsing. Suddenly, it's all he can think about.

"Ted!" I'm screaming at him to come back to me, and miraculously, he's returning to me from across some vacant lot, a cardboard box, in and out like a daydream, he's wanting to come back to me, he knows the importance. "Ted!" What can I say? "Stay with me, Ted, we have something to do, just stay with me until we get it done, please? We can do this, then you can go back to your whiskey, it's okay, you just have this one job to do. Just for today, Ted?"

"I've heard all that," he says out loud. His voice has a foggy tone to it, as if he's talking in his sleep, but it's not quite that. It's more like a daydream.

Lawrence responds, "Just let yourself be aware of your breathing."

Ted breathes in, out, deep, then deeper. His mind's in a race with his breath, and my thoughts intertwine with his, as if the two of us are competing for the Listener. "Ted! Do what he says!"—that's me speaking. Ted thinks back, "It's a waste of time, mine and yours and his too." We'll never be whole, that's what he thinks. He thinks I am the ghost of that little girl, he doesn't know who I am. He's drifting.

"Feel your breath moving into your body," Lawrence says, "feel it move through your nose, down into the lungs, hold it there, then out again, upward, and out, let all of it out, and just hold that, that emptiness, the empty chest."

"Empty your chest," is what Ted hears. He's holding his breath. He sees himself bankrupt, childless, alone. He's burning the porn, and he's emptying the bottles, and there is nothing left after that, except... me. I'm still here, swimming through the air, squeezing him—if I only could—in my endless arms, wrapping myself around and around him like cotton around a wound, making him into an empty cocoon of death and healing, helping him find his way home. He's my descendent and I love him, all his injuries and sins included, he's mine, and he hears me when I speak. I think he feels me as well—feels me hugging him—because he exhales all at once. Lawrence hears it—who couldn't—and takes a deep breath in response, knowing that Ted will hear him, monkey see, monkey do; that hearing him, Ted will breathe in and out again, a little more deeply, just because Lawrence is there listening to him and breathing with him. Lawrence is listening to Ted's silence, and all the stuff in that silence, without intruding, without knowing any of the details, without needing to know. Ted's little brown baby is safe here. But there was more than one baby. No there wasn't. To his horror, he feels wetness on his cheeks, and then a sob wants to spring out, like the gurgle of an artesian well after a drought, like a drowning person spitting the water from his lungs, coming back, splashing, unjudged, wetness nourishing everything it will touch in the summer months to come.

"Follow your breath," says Lawrence, unmoving. He doesn't turn to look at his old student, he doesn't move anything except perhaps to shift his narrow shoulders, downshifting, willing himself to remain in a calm posture, to remain an anchor, a teacher, something steady and consistent for Ted to grasp, just like Kierra holds onto Maggie, it's that same wordless spirit seeking safety, wanting to be seen and heard but only if it's safe to be seen and heard, to search for a container.

Ted breathes in and out, a little more steadily now, and loudly enough that his teacher can hear his progress. He is doing this on purpose, he's remembering now, from past experience, that Lawrence will help him monitor his breath. His big empty silence has a container to it, a container of sorts, and it's Lawrence but it's something bigger than Lawrence. A huge container is needed, something that can hold the universe.

Two more minutes tick by and that's all Ted can manage, he's standing now, tiptoeing out. He's stopped crying, but he's gone back to holding his breath. Now we're thinking again, a duet of thoughts, stereo. "Is this where Kierra should stay?" We both agree, maybe so. "Is she safer here?" We both agree, maybe so. "What about Della." What about Della? Della, who did nothing to deserve this situation, except that she married when she was in that orphan state, where you think everything is up to you, that love is eternally elusive. She was not thinking when she married; she was desperate in the way orphans are desperate. She was depressed, that is, she was alone. Now her heart is breaking, not even knowing where her child is, the child she wanted with all her heart, her first and only true love in this lifetime. It isn't fair. Ted's frowning as he escapes into the hallway that leads to the front door. He could just step outside and go on home and that would be that, but there sits Kierra, alone in a playpen while Maggie's pulling sheets out of the dryer in the laundry room. Kierra looks up at him and gasps, fearful. She's frozen there, just as Ted's been frozen the past 30 years, because she knows him and she knows it's not good, but at the same time, she KNOWS him! She smells no alcohol exuding from his very skin, and his eyes look clear—maybe it's someone else, not the Ted she vaguely knows from the other night. She can't decide. She can't move.

Ted's having the exact same experience: he's both attracted and repelled by the sight of Kierra all alone in that little baby pen, surrounded by plastic learning toys and plush animals. He could snatch her up and run, and for a moment neither one of us can decide whether that's a good idea or not. She seems secure with Maggie, and if we return her to Della the authorities will just come back and take her again. We certainly couldn't keep her, Ted and I, what oafs we would be. Let her be, Ted. Just leave it.

Lawrence has risen from his meditation cushion, following Ted, watching him. Maggie returns from the kitchen, her arms full of sheets, to look in on Kierra. From opposite sides of the living room they both catch him staring at Kierra a little too hard, a little too long, a little too silent, and they both speak at once to unlock him:

"Hey there, Ted." "Can I get you something, Ted? A drink of water?"

But Ted can't hear, and he's not even listening to me—he's remembering something that I can't tap into, and he's panicking, his heart beating in his mouth which is dry as a desert, his mind gone blank, his arms reaching—he knows they are reaching, and he knows THEY are watching, but he can't hear what they are saying—SHOUTING—as he reaches into the playpen to grab Kierra. He's got her in both arms, holding her tight, as if she might disappear into thin air, as if she won't last, as if to protect her from gunshots, and he's running, running, down the front porch steps, pushing past Thaddeus's wagging tail, down the pretty pebbly tile walkway to his car, and he's still hugging Kierra to his chest as he jumps behind the wheel and takes off down the road, Lawrence running out behind him, then running back to his own truck, then into the house for the keys. It's too late, though. By the time he's on the road, Ted's car is long gone, and Maggie only got half the license plate number scribbled on the palm of her hand with a Sharpie. Me? I'm stretched out between them, a dribble of ghostly webbing, a trail, if they could only follow it, because I am not in agreement with this. I thought Ted could hear me, if no one else, and I thought we were working this out together. Now I don't know what he's doing, and I can't look back, I have to gather myself up and away from that nice Buddhist couple, pull myself together behind Ted's ears where I can try to find out what he's got in mind. Maybe his thoughts will stop racing by the time he reaches the family cottage, and then I can catch up with what he's saying to himself, if anything is going on in that panicked, alcohol-starved brain of his.

I'm in the car now with Ted. I've left Maggie and Lawrence behind, had to. At my last glance they were on the phone with the police, and I just left, knowing whatever will happen will happen. I've seen a few generations' worth of things happening, good and bad, I'm seasoned, but I can still get the wind knocked out of my sails. You can be sure there are certain things I would like to see happen and I am not above intervening, as you know, and therefore I can be disappointed. Ted's driving too fast with that baby on his lap; if he has to stop all of a sudden she will fly out of his arms right through the windshield, so all I can say is they better not chase him, better not instigate one of those high-speed chases that never comes to any good. I'm doing my best to slow him down. Our baby's not crying, amazingly enough—but she's got her cheeks puffed out again in that funny, fluffy bird-like expression, like she's getting ready to cry or let out a sermon or both—then, when Ted screeches around a corner leaving a mark on the road and the smell of rubber in the air, she laughs outright. She laughs! And I know in that moment that she sees me, she knows there's a mother around here, and she's not afraid, even if the mother is just an old orphan ghost. How'd she get so confident? She's going to be a roller coaster girl. She laughs again as they bump up the dirt road to the family cottage in 12 minutes' time, RECORD time, and laughs more as Ted pulls the car all the way around the bumpy grass up behind the house to a one-car shed, pulls into that, and leaps out, his arms awkwardly surrounding his little grand-niece and holding her hard to his chest. How could anything bad happen with this much love in the world? Ted's dog Jeff runs down from the hillside above, barking, then wagging, and Kierra laughs yet again: she thinks it's her dog? Of course it is her dog. The world is opening up! She struggles to get down, but Ted won't let her go until they're in the house, and he lets the dog in too, seeing as they seem to know each other. He sets the baby down on the living room rug and pats her head, but she's all about the little dog. She's still not crying yet. And now Ted can hear me again. Gee whiz, he's finally listening. I help him think until he remembers she's sick, on some kind of medicine, and that he has no diapers or food suitable for a two-year-old, and he certainly can't ask me to go to the store. And if he's seen at the store with a baby and no car seat, he's sunk.

"I just want her to live," he tells me, and I murmur my sympathy to him. He's tired of things dying, that's what he's thinking; and at the same time, he's tired of living. "I need to find someone to make her well."

Unbelievable. I see it now. This is me all over again: rescued by a man and his dog, and they walked me up a hill to those brown-skinned healers who weren't afraid of...

"A witch doctor, or something like that. Somebody off the grid, that's what I need," says Ted.

"Yes," I answer. "I can see that, but they're all gone now. They burned the Mother Lovers at the stake, among other things. They burned their houses, their villages." Wait a minute, that was before my time. I must have read it somewhere in one of Della's books... because no one told me that.

More and more, I forget how I know things. At the same time, I'm knowing and knowing more and more things. I'm not sure, but I think that means I am getting closer to....

"I did not."

"No, Ted, not you. I'm talking about this country, not Viet Nam. I'm talking about a time before my lifetime, when we burned up our smart, creative women. Even when I walked the earth, back then, there were still some remnants of the Mother Lovers to be hunted down... they didn't call it that but that's what they were up to. They called it missionary work, and the like."

Ted's shaking his head like I'm crazy. "No," he says.

"I'm telling you!"

"No Granny, no. It's still happening. I've been exactly where you are talking about and I am still alive, I'm still in my body. We're still burning witches, and we can burn thousands of them all at the same time, once we have named them. Today's witches are the people of Viet Nam and the fire is napalm. Today's witches are the Pakistanis and we use drones on them."

"Ted...don't use that word. Don't say witches like that."

"I'm just putting it out there. 'Mother Lovers.' I know."

"Names are important, Ted."

"I know. But listen, that's where we need to go: Viet Nam. I got a credit card, do they take babies on airplanes? Do you know, I mean, can I hold her on my lap?"

"Viet Nam? I don't think I can get off of this continent. I'm... not allowed." But that is a lie. To be honest, all that water scares me, I don't think I would make it. So I give him some advice I have yet to take. "You're living in the past, Ted, and I am here to tell you the past is dead, whether it is 400 years old or 40. We'll have to use the resources available now, something local."

Truth is I'm terrified; never in my lifetime, nor in my ghost-time, have I been anywhere near that deep deep body of water known as the ocean, the first lady of secrets, the twilight body of other worlds.

"There are some pagans living in the trailer park."

"I don't know what that is."

"Pagans. Witches—I mean, Mother Lovers. They do ceremonies up the mountain, on the full moon or whatever."

"No, I mean, 'trailer park.' What's that?"

"Oh, that. I can't explain it, it's like living in tin boxes only the boxes are big, big enough for a whole family. They line them up in rows."

"I get that. You mean mobile homes, son. Do they do healing?"

"Eh?"

"Pagans. Your modern-day Mother Lovers. Do they know anything about healing, real healing? I thought that was lost over the last hundred years or so." I'm still wringing my hands over that ocean thing.

"There's one, an old lady, she'll lay her hands and pray. I saw her do it to some buddies of mine. She's kind of like Jesus, up on the mountain praying, all by herself up there."

I'm skeptical. "Baptist?"

"No, s'matter of fact, she's just a mix of everything, and I'll bet she's a hundred years old. She's not some fundamentalist—if that's what you're worrying about. But it's a problem. She don't live nearby, she's up the other direction, north of here, forty miles or so on the border with Tennessee. And she can be cranky."

"That's the best we've got, then let's go."

"We'll have to walk. I can get us on the Appalachian Trail and get us to my healer friend that way, but it'll take a couple of days, maybe three, walking, but the trail, once we get on it, it goes right past Ol' Granny's house and they keep that trail cleared. I did it once before."

"What about Della?" he hears that loud and clear. Kierra's good temper is not going to last long, especially as night approaches; without even Maggie to mother her, she'll be wanting her real mother, wanting her bad.

"You go get Della, have her meet me on the trail, then we'll walk together to the old lady's hut. It's uphill by the way."

"Surely Ol' Granny has a name."

"Yeah. Ol' Granny."

"Ol' Granny who?"

"Granny, just Granny, Ol' Granny Apple is what they say."

"Don't be silly."

"Okay, some people call her Mom."

"Mom. Okay then. I'll go for Della now, it'll take some work."

"I'll get my boots on. Kierra and me, we'll head down the creek as far as we can take it, just in case they try some old-fashioned tracking. I heard they've been training hounds down at the county, because I was thinking about training Jeff the Dog for that kind of work. Mmm...." (He's looking for his socks.) "The trail passes not too far from Della's house, maybe a mile. She can drive if she don't want to hike it. Just don't have her parking her car too close to the trail, have her leave it at the Ingles. Got that?"

"Got it." Now I'm taking instructions from a human, but frankly, Ted's half something else, always has been, I swear I saw it in him at birth.

One thing on my side: Della can hear me. Sometimes.

I hate to leave them. Ted's so clumsy, but at least he's sober. He's got the baby tied up in a sort of a homemade papoose on his back, and he's found out she can pee pee on the potty, which means the diaper she has on will last a bit longer than it would otherwise, if he can just remember to tell her to go every hour or so. He's figuring things out. He's fashioned a little backpack for Jeff the Dog—of course Jeff will go with them—and he's stuffed that with candy bars and peanut butter and crackers, and iodine so they can drink the creek water. In the short run, Kierra can eat those things. It's something, better than nothing. As I leave I can see that she's doing okay with him, and I have to admit he is a different person when he's not drinking. Not just that he's sober, there's more to it, he's really somebody else, another him, bright-eyed, enthusiastic, hopeful, smart. Right now Ted's full of energy, and his mind is working well as he organizes his trip to meet up with Della, then on to Granny's place. It's a strange, wiry, electric energy.

If I can just get through to Della, make her understand what she needs to do, because she's not going to want to do it.

    I'm flying fast, leaping across time, across two coves and one creek that's big enough to be a river in the springtime. I'm weaving in and out of existence, and if you're driving you'll see me, sometimes, if you look up—I am that thin fog about 15 feet off the ground, that thin layer you see, usually at dusk, around these particular mountains. Trust me, it's not fog. When you see it, you feel a friendly feeling, and that's because it is. It's friendly. Don't ever be afraid of fog, especially at night.

    I fly along the lay lines, many of them covered now in pavement and cars, motorcycles, trucks, fire engines, bikes, but very few walkers and even the deer steer clear, cutting through the woods instead. You'll see an occasional dog skittering down the road, evading the new county law about leashes and fences, drinking up his last long drink of freedom before everything is "civilized," even our mountain hounds, even these very mountains. Maybe the mountains—being somewhat bigger than us—can hold out, like that handful of the Cherokee who lingered in caves and crevices instead of walking to that desert, Oklahoma. Like the mountains, those particular people were giants among us.

THIRTEEN

Sure, I like to think that these mountains will always be here, because I myself may be here for the duration of the human species if I don't pull this off with Della.

I can't say where I lost the time, but it's late afternoon. I'm at the back door, but it's locked. Della's inside crying. Tommy's gone off to play cards because that's what he does when he's upset. Cynthia's cooking something for dinner, and running cold water over a washcloth to put on Della's head. Della's letting her do that. GOOD. Be mothered, Della, it's never too late and there's no shame in it. You see, that's another one of the orphan things: when we have an opportunity for mothering we shun it, we practically feel shamed by it. We turn our face away from it. No girls' week at the beach for us. No advice from Mama for us. No taking a time out. No pampering at the spa—that's for girly girls, who for some reason enjoy having their toenails painted.

For tonight, Cynthia puts the wash rag on her daughter's forehead, and her daughter just lies there on the sofa, letting her mother cook, contemplating the impossible notion of actually eating something. It's a start. I see it all through the windows but I can't get in. It's as if Della can only allow one mother at a time and she's shutting me out so she can let Cynthia in. This won't do.

I try all the doors, find none of them cracked even a little. Maybe it's Tommy they're shutting out? I fumble at the upstairs window, that little vent that goes into the crawl space that one day will be refinished into a bedroom. Even that won't budge. I'm swirling around and around, pressing on the very walls, whining at them like a soft stormy wind, begging Della to hear me. Nothing. She doesn't want me, she's shutting me out, she's shutting down. The sun is setting, who knows how far Ted's gotten with his make-shift family—Kierra and Jeff the Dog—walking down the side of that mountain, him with his rain shoes on so that he can slog right through the creek, which is full of slippery rocks and other hazards. Has he dropped the baby yet? Is she hypothermic from falling straight into the water, or has she been knocked out by a rock? No. I know she's not, because I can feel all three of them in my heart, my spiritual green hazy heart, I feel them walking, moving. There is movement, and that is good, because Ted has not walked a straight path since he came home from Viet Nam.

I have time, but not much.

I bang against the window, willing sound to happen, and finally Cynthia looks up. She stares, suspicious, at the window. She walks to it, startles at her own reflection, almost sees me. She shakes off her fear. "It'll be okay," she says, the Mother's Mantra, it's something we say whether it is true or not, whether it will be okay or not. We have to say it, or who else will? She sets the cool washrag on Della's head and falls, with a heavy sigh, into the recliner beside her daughter.

"It's okay NOW," I whisper, but it comes out as a faint, small screeching sound, a birdlike noise, and now both of them look up.

"Was that an owl?" asks Della. "That was a weird noise." She sits up, throws the washcloth onto the coffee table, walks to the window, opens it. Here's my chance, I could slip in—but she slams it shut as I'm coming through, cutting off my toes. (That's okay, they grow right back.) I fall in, a little piece of mist hitting the carpet. I follow Della back to the sofa where she lies back down, her hand to her head. She's shutting me out. I'm stomping on her, no good, shouting in her ear and she only turns her head. She's restless with her own thoughts and she can barely even see her own mother puttering about in the kitchen. She's hot and unhappy. She hops up and opens the window again to let in the cool dark breeze, and I'm right behind her, and from here I can see what she cannot—that wild river otter making her way along the path up to the back of the house. I twirl around Della's shoulders and spin out into the night.

Ms. Otter is on her night patrol, exploring beneath the house, disappearing into the cave-like crawl space that Tommy keeps saying he'll close in and insulate before winter. For now it's wide open, and there she is, that river otter, rooting about underneath the house. Her humped back makes her look like an old lady cat as she feels her way around in the dim light using her whiskers as a guide. I'm following her every step. I come up behind her, fast. Our eyes meet. Here we are, Granny Ghost and Mama Otter, and we both know what's going to happen next. Now I remember the hole in the wall of the bathroom closet—and I don't even have to ask; I just climb up onto her back, cling hard, until we're one. (I've only done this once before; it's very powerful, but it takes a lot out of me.) Together, as one, we climb back into the house where that gap in the bathroom closet remains unmended—who wants to do carpentry when social services has your child?—and we're up, inside the house. It's hard not to stop and sniff around at the pool of water where Della dripped when she got out of the bath late this afternoon, but we pass it up to go directly into the living area. Slowly. Take it easy, River Otter, we can't spook them, not quite yet. We need Della to follow us out of the house, not chase us back into the bathroom closet.

Della's reading something, or pretending to read. We're sniffing around the sofa when Cynthia comes slamming across the room.

"What're you doing, Mom?"

"You didn't latch that window. I am latching it." Then her mother screams, "The rat! Oh! The rat! It's back!"

I can't get loose. The otter and I are one, running in circles, trying to find a way to escape, because the otter's nature has taken over, I have no control. She's making a bee-line back to the bathroom now, Della and Cynthia standing, frozen, open-mouthed. After one second, Della follows to see where we went, wanting to figure out how that animal keeps getting into the house. She follows quickly enough to see our back end disappearing into the closet, and she flings the door all the way open, pushes aside some towels, and sure enough, there's the hole. It's big enough for a bear cub to get through. She didn't know it was there, that tells you how much of a housekeeper we are, me and my descendents. Frankly, I've come to prefer the outdoors, entirely.

We're out of the house, mission not accomplished. The Lady Otter and I sit beside the creek, preening ourselves. What to do. There's light, and the sound of some kind of comforting music,

Enya, I believe, coming from the house. Movement past windows. The sound of voices debating. Then Della steps out the door onto the back steps and scans her small grass yard, which is mostly weeds and twigs, but some grass where the sun hits it.

"I'll be right back, Mom."

"That rat is not a sign."

"It's an otter, Mom, the same one that was here the other night."

"Same as a rat, belongs outside, leave it alone. It might have rabies."

"I'll be right back."

Della's walking straight towards us, and that is a good sign indeed. She's onto something. She's listening to me. "Hello?" she calls. "Anyone out there?"

"Yes! Yes!" I'm screaming loud now, and sounding very much like a screech owl. This gives Della hope, and she continues walking straight at us, and I'm willing the Otter not to move, we are still one and I need Ms. River Otter to hold her ground, go against her nature and meet the human face to face. Sure enough, she rises onto her back legs, our little paws are in the air, slightly folded, the closest an otter can come to crossing her arms. If she could tap her foot, we would.

Della comes to a dead stop, not because of us but because she can't see a thing. Right here is where the darkness of the woods begins to take over. She has to let her eyes adjust. There, there, she's seeing, she's seeing.

"Here! Here!" I'm shouting with all my might.

Her eyes lock into our eyes and the three of us are one. River Otter jerks her head to the right, as if pointing, and we're off—all three of us. Hallelujah, Della's joined us. She's scrambling up the creek. Too bad we couldn't tell her to bring food, a sleeping bag, some iodine to kill the germs in the creek water she's going to have to drink. Only now do I begin to realize what bad timing this is—Ted's only just started out, it'll take him hours to reach this part of the trail. Della's likely to give up, if she stops to think that she's out here in the woods with nothing.

But the funny thing is, she seems to like being out here, alone in the darkening woods, alone and foodless. She hums "Moon River," as she walks along the path that leads up to the

Appalachian Trail. She knows where she is, the moon is rising, the path wide, and the way things are in her life she could walk forever, into another life, a new time. Why go home?

I fly ahead to find out how much progress Ted's made. I find him still two miles off, as best I can estimate, but he's trudging like a trooper, stomping ever onward, holding onto Kierra like she's a lump of gold, and all the while the little dog Jeff trotting beside them with a little dog smile on her face. At the moment, Kierra's too curious to be afraid, and Ted's strong arms and Jeff's happy tail keep her feeling safe, safe enough to just look around. Kierra's night vision is good. She's in her element here in the woods. I would say she's like her mother in this way, she's got the wood spirit in her, and for the moment, she's content. When Ted stops for dinner and pulls out candy and peanut butter, she's actually happy. She's licking her fingers, then sticking them out for Jeff the Dog to lick, then putting them back in her mouth. Ted doesn't notice things like that. He's behind a tree peeing, fighting back any second-guessing.

The police left Lawrence and Maggie's house hours ago, their notepads full of notes, their computers updated, a picture of Ted in all hands, and they've tracked down some information on his old Volkswagen, and they've been looking for Ted. I don't understand why they're just now on their way to Della's house—it seems like she'd be the first one they would call. I'm guessing they hoped to find her baby first.

There's an Amber Alert on the radio. I have to wonder how it might have been for me, under that rock, if they'd had an Amber Alert for me and somehow I think it would've been worse. Someone "good" might've taken me in.

The police arrive at Della's less than 10 minutes after her departure into the woods. Cynthia, suspicious of everything, tells them a lie: her daughter's gone into town for groceries, might stay in town for a movie.

"Isn't that her car?" asks Officer Laughter. "That Buick out there?"

"Yessir," replies Cynthia. "She took mine."

"Describe it."

"Why do you need to know?"

"We can't—" says Officer Laughter, but Officer Trantham interrupts, "We can tell her. It's about Della's daughter, Kierra. Ted Potter's run off with her, kidnapped her."

"Oh hell."

"Yes," says Officer Trantham. "That's what we're dealing with."

"Ah, hm." Now she's sorry she lied. "It's a red car. I... rented it. Um, a Chevy, some type of Chevy. I don't know cars."

"Where'd you rent it from?"

"Oh I can't even think right now. Tell you what, when she's back I'll have her call you, okay? I don't know what else to say. Except I can tell you Ted's no pedophile, if that's what you're thinking."

"In all due respect, ma'am, family members are generally the last to know when it comes to that."

"He has a heart of gold."

"We hear that all the time."

Cynthia slams the door in their faces. Fuming, she paces the living room. Then she remembers her daughter has a cell phone, so she calls her daughter. There is a jarring sound of wind chimes—Della's phone, ringing right there on the coffee table.

○

Tiring, Della sits down on the nearest rock. Out of the corner of her eye... she sees us. Ms. Otter and I have followed her, to give her our moral support, and to see that she keeps moving. You see, that's the key in situations like this, you've got to keep moving, that will help you keep thinking up new ideas. If you sit still, hide in the house, get bogged down, you start to think in circles. You get afraid. You think you have to figure out just exactly the right thing to do before you can take another step, so you never take another step, and they'll bury you in that condition. DO YOU HEAR ME? Keep moving, like the river otter, like the spirits that live in these woods.

Sure enough, Della sees us, and what does she do? She stands up, she's got her hand to her throat, and there's a smile, a real genuine smile, which I have not seen on Della's face since she was a baby. See? I nudge the otter, I hug the otter, even though we are still one being, she can feel my hug, and Della can almost see it. See? We're helping. We're pushing Della down the path. Sure enough, she's knowing what to do next. Instead of pursuing us, she gazes at us, with appreciation, stopping all other thought, until a new thought finds her, tells her to walk the trail. Head in the direction of the family cabin. You hiked it once, it goes straight over there. No, she's not aware that Ted's on his way, she's strictly going on her intuition, and Mother Otter can take the credit for that.

Meanwhile, Tommy's finishing up his card game and reluctantly moving toward the door of Alvin's apartment, and Finn is asking if he'd like to stay over, have another beer maybe, and Tommy's forming the words "why not" when he gets the call from Cynthia.

"I had to call," she says, "but this isn't a call I want to make."

"What now?"

"Your baby's missing. Ted's got her."

"WHAT?"

"Ted took her out of the foster placement. Kidnapped her. They don't know where he is, but he's got her."

"Is he drunk?"

"They say he wasn't drunk at the time, not obviously anyway. But that's all we know."

"That asshole. Let me talk to Della."

"She's not here."

"Oh, what, is she with the police?"

"No, they came by here looking for her, but she isn't here."

"Where is she?"

"Honestly? I don't know, Tommy. I don't know."

"Then what am I supposed to do? Do you want me to come home?"

"Do whatever you need to do, Tommy. I just had to call."

"When you see Della, tell her to call me. I'm not going anywhere, I've had three beers and I don't need to run into any trouble with all of this sh—this stuff going on. You tell her to call me. Tell her to call me."

"Okay, Tommy."

"Tell her."

"I will."

Tommy turns off his ringer, without really thinking about it, because that's what he does when he stays late at Finn's, it's just a habit. He's offline now, drinking the fourth beer, and stopping after finishing half of it, because he's starting to feel sad, flat out sad. Della's too good for him—it's a fleeting thought—and he's tired of trying, and some part of him likes the idea of being free of family life. When he was growing up, it was never any fun, so why did he think his own family would be different, when he attempted it? I'm swirling through his mind, tasting his thoughts, and they're oddly sweet.

He falls straight asleep on Finn's sofa, but he'll be up around 2am, I know, I've witnessed it every night, he'll be up and unable to go back to sleep. Probably, by 3am or 4am, he'll be in his car, on his way back home. He'll be up early for work; whenever there's stress in the family, he works harder, he really does. That, and cards, and pot, and sometimes, church. These are the things that help Tommy cope.

Mr. Pearson calls, and since Della signed a release, he talks with Cynthia for half an hour or so. The bruises were verified as most likely being related to the cancer, not abuse. The river rat, or otter, depending on who you ask, was deemed a one-time event, not an ongoing risk factor. And Uncle Ted was not a frequent visitor to the home, in fact, the opposite. "But now, as I said, all bets are off. The case is frozen until Kierra is found. I need to ask about that man, Ted Potter, Della's uncle. Your brother, right? What kind of person is he? I understand he's had several DUI's here in the county, over the past 20 years, and that alone is very concerning."

"He's an alcoholic, yes."

"Anything else?"

"Like I told the police, he keeps away from children, if that's what you're asking. He doesn't go after kids, doesn't even have any of his own. Della says he hasn't been around to visit since Kierra was a year old. He likes dogs, that's about it, he always has a dog or two. He's on disability for his PTSD, goes to the VA sometimes for counseling, but he dropped that a few years ago, as far as I know."

"Do you think Kierra's safe?"

"God only knows. Ted wouldn't hurt her on purpose,

that's all I can tell you. He has a good heart. He's been a vegetarian for... maybe, five, ten years, I think. That's a little strange, but otherwise..."

"I'm sorry, someone just walked into my office. Can I call you again?"

"Please do."

Cynthia's sipping a glass of wine, but it isn't working. Instead, she's getting a headache. She leans her head down into her arms and rests like that, her wine glass and soup bowl pushed aside. Della still hasn't returned, and there are bears. Also, Della ran out without a coat, and it gets cold at night here in the mountains. And what about Ted? Those telephone questions set Cynthia to thinking, how Ted suddenly became a vegetarian—out of everything else in his life that was the one thing he's stuck with to this day. It had something to do with a meditation class he took out at the VA, he really liked the teacher, but he didn't keep up with the class. He said meditation didn't help him, made him feel crazier, actually. But he liked the teacher, held him in high esteem for some reason.

Cynthia knows where he is, she made him go there—out to the family cabin—and there's no doubt in her mind that he's taken Kierra up there, where else could he go? And she never asked, how did he kidnap Kierra when he had no car keys? Ohhh.... The obvious hits her. How could she be so stupid?

But how did he figure out Kierra's location? And where's Della gone, is she in on it? All of this smashes into her brain at once, it feels like a banana split on a full stomach, it makes her feel crazy, sick, and now the migraine is chugging towards her like a freight train. She knows what to do, what she has to do. There's no other choice but to lie down in the dark for an hour with a cold rag over her eyes. Then, if she's able, she'll get up, buy a pack of Marlboro's, and go see about Ted in the family cabin. She'll take some diapers along, she'll figure out what to do when she finds them. That's the plan. She turns all the lights out in the house. She soaks the washcloth in ice water. She doesn't remember falling asleep.

FOURTEEN

At 1am Della's also finally drowsing, having crawled into a rock crevice and raked up a cushion of pine needles all around herself for insulation. She doesn't care how she'll look in the morning, she doesn't care how she'll look for the rest of her life; her baby is gone from her. She hasn't run into Ted yet, but that little otter won't give up, she lingers behind, forges ahead, watches from a distance. Because of the otter, Della's not afraid. At 3am she wakes at the sound of someone's bad dream—a wail of sorts—it could be the screech owl, or it could have been herself. At least it did not sound like a child, but then again… could it be? She's sitting up, completely awake, listening, but there's no sound at all. The moon's high, and the otter's grey back glistens almost out of view beneath a clump of rhododendrons. As Della's eyes adjust to the dim light she can see the soft furry movement of breath, gentle, peaceful breath. She's not afraid—after all, the otter's sound asleep—that awful sound, it must have been a dream, so she thinks, and she wills herself to close her eyes, she counts her breath, she counts sheep, she sleeps.

But it was me calling out. I'm with my granddaughter Elizabeth—Della's grandma—she's trying to leave this world but it's slow going when you have Alzheimer's. She's come to see me, to hold my hand, and I am time-traveling with her. She's looking for something she lost. She's going back, back, back, one day, one week, one year at a time, each day like a card in an infinite deck, each one crystal clear and in color. She has gotten herself all snagged up on the day George Bright Apple died, so she's come to see me about it. He was her best friend from the 7th grade and all through high school, a transplant from one county over. I can remember George well, there was something about him. You could tell he came from wealth, or education, or both, and something wild thrown in. Elizabeth was crazy over his straight black hair, green eyes and his perfect speech, all of which he got from his mother, so he said—his mother with the lavender diamond ring and the crystal ball (so he said). Elizabeth loved every bit of him and she pined to meet his mother, a hermit widow holed up in her home place up towards Johnson City, Tennessee. Elizabeth thought she could draw that woman out, but that never happened. Yes, it's all come back to me, especially the part about the ring, because I was still a little envious of such things back then.

She cries out at that memory, her George lost in the war. She screams only because it was buried so deep and now out of the blue it's caught her like a heavy hook in fresh flesh. But that's not when I cried out like a screech owl, waking Della. My own hollering, that came a few moments later.

Amy Ellen Elizabeth, my dear granddaughter, such a beauty inside and out. She's finally finding her way home, she's almost, almost shed of her body, and she's come to me in her dreams to show me the obituary she saved all her life. Why now? Why wait until now to tell me? It's because I'm on the move. I'm up here on this trail, and Della is with me, and Cynthia watching out at the house, and Kierra approaching. We are all together and moving, and nothing will ever be the same. I am telling you.

○

I couldn't read, back then, when I was still in the body. I never saw the write-up in the Johnson City paper. But I was there for Elizabeth when George died. I knew she secretly loved him, I held her while she cried and she knew I understood, having lost my Thomas so many years before. But that girl was restless. Within a month after his death she'd moved somewhere up north in order to pass as white, brushing out her tracks behind her so nobody from her past could follow.

Yes, I remember, though I don't like to. George Apple died in the war, the second big war, who knows how he died, exactly. They gave us a story on the telephone, and that's all we had left of George, back home, a story. By the time I died, the war was over and Elizabeth had been gone from us for almost six years.

She must have taken the obituary with her. It's... where.... I see it, it's in Emily's cookbook, the one I gave my daughter for her wedding. There in the obituary Elizabeth has underlined George's lineage and I'm reading it, nothing else to do, and it hits me smack in the left side of my head, it hits me hard when I see it so clear and plain, spelled out in the newspaper, that George was Elizabeth's own distant cousin, my own great-nephew, and we didn't know it. Generations later I am still discovering so much! To think, my nephew George ate pecan pie in my kitchen. They held hands, George Bright Apple and my Elizabeth. He was the last of his line, only that hermit mother—she would have been my niece—surviving him. No doubt she's long gone by now, the niece I never met, along with her ring and her crystal ball.

I wish I'd had a crystal ball, just to hold it, that's all. Reminds me of a baby's head, and beauty, and hope.

All the way out there on the west coast, in her nursing home bed, Elizabeth calls out in her sleep, yelling as if she has just got the call: George is GONE. I'm the only one left to hear her, since she's travelled so far from her own body, about as far as you can go and still be living. I've read the news, I've looked up at Elizabeth and said, "is it true?" and she's nodded at me, and she's crying again, and that's when I shrieked from sheer pleasure and sheer disbelief, shouting out to the world, waking Della. Although I didn't know it at the time I had a niece, and a great-nephew, and I had the privilege to meet the nephew in person, again and again, back there then. I hugged him goodbye when he shipped out. As for Elizabeth, her grief won't last, she'll go further back in time, to a time when George still lived, to the time they met, and to a time before they met.

The truth is, everything's happening at once.

I'm following Elizabeth back into the womb, into her mother and through me myself, back another generation, then another, to a faraway time and place on the other side of the ocean. I know these people—a black-haired, freckled, fair-skinned folk. They belong to the earth, having farmed it many centuries, having uprooted many a rock to make a field. Working in silence by day, they sing at night. They lift their noses to smell the salt air, and that's not arrogance, it's love. One of them, nameless now, sailed to the New World in a small boat, gave birth to a tiny girl in a dark damp room below deck. She stepped off the vessel a young mother full of hope only to be killed three years later because, now I see it, she had the crossed eye, she had the gift. She left behind her three-year-old daughter.

We are the offspring of that nameless orphan, Della. Crows, moonbeams, mountain dogs and river otters watch over us. Them, and the occasional bobcat, and once in a while, a bear.

I've called out!, loud!, my own helpless echo of Elizabeth's grief, my disbelief and my pleasure, and together with all our racket we woke Della up. Maybe that's what Elizabeth came for—to wake up Della, but also to tell me about George—this seems to have satisfied her, because now, my Elizabeth, my dear granddaughter— she's taking my hand. She wants to leave her treasure trunk of memories behind, and fly. She squeezes my hand, and she's gone, just like that. She's passed.

Go back to sleep, Della. Nothing will ever be the same, yet here we still are.

In my own endless wakefulness, I have sighted Ted a mile off, walking steady as a robot, as if he had no end to his energy source, whatever it might be, with that baby asleep on his back in a make-shift backpack, and his dog trodding along behind, drooping her spindly tail, but keeping her chin up and her eyes open. Good. There's determination heading towards us, there's hope in that little dog, and in the human as well (I am talking about a particular human that everyone had given up on, including Ted himself, yes Ted gave up on himself, and now it seems as though some young stranger inhabits his body). Such a difference between drunk and sober, it's like the expanse between five generations, the divide between sleep and wakefulness. He's strong, focused and free. He almost can't stand it; it's as if he watches himself completing this task, even though he's the one doing it, he's watching it, and he's not really in his body anymore. If he lets himself worry, it will be about the consequences and the EXPECTATIONS to come. He feels like an acrobat on a thin line, and there's nothing to do but go forward. And the terrible restlessness. He's almost become a ghost like me, but no you don't Ted, not yet. He's past sleepiness. He's past the desire for whiskey, at least for now. There's no hunger rumbling in his stomach. Someone brave, someone heroic has taken over his weary body, someone Kierra unabashedly likes. It's an adrenaline rush. It's fear, and it's conviction.

So much change is happening it could scare someone to death if they dared to realize it. So Ted walks onward, unthinking, and Della goes back to sleep, convincing herself she did not hear a ghost. They know not what they do, and this is why Ted can keep walking, and Della can keep sleeping. Soon—just after daybreak—they'll be able to trade places. Ted will sleep-walk, Della will walk carrying Kierra, her dream come true. They'll go on to the next place. This is the way they'll keep this strange little freedom train moving, by trading places, shape-shifting. Their destination? Ted will be free of his addiction to alcohol, even if it kills him, and Della will be free of her addiction to Tommy, no matter how many stones he throws.

As for me, I'll be free of my remaining ghostly strands of silken thread that hold me to this place of density—with all its beauty and misery—and most of all, finally, last but not least, my great-great-great-granddaughter, this child of mine named Kierra? She will grow up knowing beyond all doubt what it means to be free. She'll have not one mother, but three.

○

But I get ahead of myself, which is not hard to do the way I'm stretching and thinning all over the place, becoming the thinnest of fogs almost to the point that I am, sometimes, a mere transient mist of dew coating the wildflowers. It takes more and more effort to materialize. I'm grateful to Lady Otter for allowing me to piggyback on her. I don't know why she's allowed it, because we don't share a common language, and the light behind our eyes is so very different. Still, here we are. We communicate.

When Della's finally drifted back into a truly sound sleep, Ms. Otter and I gingerly step up, stretch, look around. We were never really sleeping; we had one eye open the whole time. Now we'll move forward again, up the trail, meeting Ted, giving him a small booster shot of hope, and giving Jeff the Dog something to chase—nothing like a wild otter to wake up that doggie, if she was getting tired or bored. What a treat, and you know Ms. Otter will hiss and snap as she flees back into the creek, then she'll flow on down 'round the rocks and bends, the deep and the shallow, back to the French Broad where she came from, where she belongs. We're moving fast as a team, and though I'm tired of this existence, I still love it at times like this. I love the feeling of wild competence, the lack of fear, the life in those muscular legs and the wiry whiskers that seem to know everything. I love the absence of speech and the presence of knowing. I love the feeling of physical movement as we walk, then step it up a bit, then run—run like the wind—head on towards Ted and his dog and our sleeping baby. It's like a homecoming, all at once, the most marvelous party I've ever attended, because suddenly I realize we are heading straight for those hemlocks where I gave up my body so many generations ago. All at once I know that we'll meet exactly there, on that spot, which is now just flat ground, no trace of anything. The hemlocks, though—oh, they've been dying in these parts, dying in a plague that wants to wipe them all out—the wooly adelgid, that invisible animal, has been taking them down one by one in spite of chemicals, in spite of massive releases of ladybugs to eat them up. So I'm sad, and I'm cautioning myself, but, yes, we're coming up on them now—and I SEE them, they're still intact, miraculously, I see, they are still robust, green, still sheltering the salamander and the flying squirrel, still keeping life alive. We have to stop so I can get off, and prostrate myself, Thank the Hemlock for being, still. For now. Thank you.

Next thing I see: Ted coming through the trees, stomping up the path that leads straight through here, his blue eyes intent on everything as if he never slept, never in his existence. He is just blue eyes, staring. That's what, that's who appears before us. A pair of eyes, like headlights in fog. He's looking right at me. Jeff the Dog's not far behind, and when she catches the otter's scent, they're off. I have to laugh. Not even a goodbye, but that's okay, we don't have each other's language anyway, and it's all understood from the start. The timeless chase. Thank you, Lady Otter. Don't go too far, yet! You'll swim in the French Broad soon enough.

Ted stares at me, then slumps to his knees as if I might catch him, and next thing you know he's on the ground, barely awake. Sleep did catch up to him, and the timing is not perfect because Della's still asleep, several yards off, close, but no use to us here. If Kierra remains asleep we'll be okay. Maybe I can help cover her with the little bit of me that remains after all the effort of that work with the otter and all the generations before now. Maybe Kierra would recognize my scent, would accept me as a substitute blanket, thin and torn, but familiar enough.

But that's not necessary: Jeff the Dog is back, unsuccessful in her hunt. Otter's long gone, as far as Jeff is concerned, and now Jeff's circling us, panting happily. She flops down on the other side of Kierra, who has slouched off Ted's back onto the soft ground, so now Kierra's sandwiched between the two of them, and what a trooper—even though I see Kierra open her eyes, waking briefly to yet another unknown place and time, still she keeps her mouth closed, and next thing, she's blinked herself back to sleep. Maybe she's just that tired, but it's as if she knows her mother is coming, and all is well. Maybe that's because I told her, I sang it to her with the wind as my background accompaniment.

MOTHER IS COMING.

ALL IS WELL.

MOTHER IS COMING.

ALL IS WELL.

MOTHER IS COMING.

ALL IS WELL.

Maybe she can hear me, just like the otter, even though our language is so different, me an aging ghost, she a fresh being full to bursting with life, with the water and sparkle of life.

I know, you think I say things funny. I don't care. Kierra understands. She hears things you don't, and she understands how I talk, she understands completely, and that's how it is when things are working full-tilt to their full potential. You'll see. The water. The sparkle.

FIFTEEN

The police in this town are not a joke. No. Many of them are very smart, and they take their jobs seriously, and they do have a respect for differences, including gays and lesbians, Russians, Cherokees, undocumented immigrants, the descendents of slaves, poor whites, Northerners, and next-door neighbors. Excuse me if I left anybody out. These police, they've made it a point to become familiar with the multitude of religions and spiritual practices that are popping up, a new one every other day, in these mountain places where sky and earth rub noses. There are both men and women on the police force these days, and various shades of skin, not just white, quite a change from my days, and they are both young and old and everything in the middle. I do appreciate them when they're able to do a bit of good, especially for the newcomers, and people who are different. I also know they will not give up on this hunt. I also know that the local newspaper, always snooping for sensation, has already posted this story on the front page and tomorrow Della will lose her job.

Tommy has a friend or two on the force, and this disaster has revved him up. Suddenly his child is the most important thing. It's his beautiful child, and yes, he does love Kierra even if he's always been content to let her raise herself. He does! When it comes to children, he just doesn't see a need beyond three meals and a bed to sleep in, he lets Della fuss around doing more than that, but it's a waste of energy—it's neurotic, in his book—and he tries not to get involved with all that. He does, however, enjoy the adrenaline of a tragedy, the dramatic idea of being the stricken dad who will not stop until his daughter is found, and indeed, if he ever finds her, he'll play that part for at least a week, maybe a month or two. He will play it well, and at first he'll mean it. Then he'll see about suing somebody. Fact is, he does love his kid.

He really does.

○

In other words, it's beginning to look like Della must stay in the woods, maybe forever. She's better off here. She must find Ted, of course, so that she can be reunited with Kierra and they can stick together. I'm whispering these instructions in her ear while she sleeps, hoping some or most of it will "take" and she'll wake up knowing what to do. She needs to stick with her uncle. Ted knows how to get along in the woods, he thinks well in the woods, when his body is moving and he's not drinking. Ted doesn't pretend that he likes children, but he does, in his own way. He avoids children because he doesn't want to harm them, and after his experience with war he figures that's all he's good for, harming the unarmed, but even so, he does care about people, and their children, and he's tired of his regrets. It's time to move forward.

He knows that if he's found, he'll be in more trouble than ever, way more than he can talk his way out of, so he must not be found. Ever. Ted has a destination in mind, and it is a destination way off the beaten track. I catch glimpses of it. There's a part of him wants to die, but not before he gets his people to Granny's. And the part of him that wants to live is always talking back.

"Why does life go on?" he asks.

"Because it is so beautiful," Ol' Granny replies. How can he argue.

○

There will be someone there to receive them, if he can find Della, and if Ol' Granny's still living. If they come upon only her bones up there, well then, maybe some of her medicine still lingers in her cabin. It's the only solution he can think of, having set his feet in motion and carried the little girl with him. He means no harm, let me emphasize that. I see more and more clearly the longer I stick around this world, I can pick out the mean ones and the kind ones pretty fast.

Della and Ted and Jeff the Dog and Kierra are all fast asleep, closer to each other than they could possibly imagine, and the sun's rising in the sky. I hear sirens down in the valley, but that's probably an ambulance; I try not to worry. Police in search of runaways don't advertise themselves like that. Still, it bothers me. I feel their presence, I know they are searching tirelessly, and the Amber alert gets everyone involved. There are plenty of hikers around these parts, but at least it is a weekday, when they're less likely to be this far out. The point is, the day is dawning, and I have to wake somebody up, and that'll be Della—she's had about four hours' sleep, which is pretty good for being out in the woods without a sleeping bag.

I'm tired myself. My wispy body stretches out like a salamander along the ground and I slither, like that, smooth and invisible, over to Della's homemade sleeping cave. I tickle her nose mercilessly, until she sneezes, once, a small sneeze. I tickle again, and again, nothing. So I take all my strength and ball it up into a puffball of otter fluff, yes, otter fluff—grey, downy, sticky—and throw it full-tilt at her little white nose. Ahh… ahhh…. Ahhh….

"CHOO!" She's awake.

"Della."

"What?" She's looking around, squinting, a hand to her forehead. "What?"

"Della, listen."

"Ohhhh what am I doing? Where's my baby?"

"Della!!"

Suddenly she stiffens, listening, as if sniffing the air to smell any sound, any sight, any smell that might tell her what to do next. The forest is empty, though, like her heart. She's trying too hard. She's not listening.

"DELLA!!!"

She barely hears me.

Then, a wail, that seems to come from Della's very heart—her mouth is not moving—it isn't her, it's some spirit, some unhappy being, an elf or a bear cub—no, no… it is our very own two-year-old Kierra, straight down the path from Della and just a little to the left, in the bend by the big rock, our little Kierra is wide awake, upright, and toddling along now, Jeff at her side nipping at her feet, trying to get her to turn around and go back to Ted, who lies on the ground, still knocked out deep asleep, in that little cove beside the trail, his eyes cracked open slightly like a dead man. Kierra doesn't like Ted when Ted is asleep. She's scared and angry. Ms. Otter's returned, but keeping a safe distance, walking lightly so as not to alert Jeff the Dog and engage in another running match. Ms. Otter's willing Kierra along, blessing her, sending her the right way, towards Della. Thank you again, Mama Otter, your intuition is so strong and pure. Thank you for circling back to us; I know your heart is hungry for the French Broad River.

Kierra's walking and crying at the same time, not knowing she's being led, but moving along just the same.

"Kierra!" That's Della.

Della's running faster than she's ever run in her life, even when she was 12 and won the 100 yard sprint. Her hips are moving like pistons, the sweat of centuries of sleep and dreams flying off her neck. Nobody cares what Della looks like as she grabs her daughter and hugs her almost to the point of mutual suffocation. Part One of my mission has been achieved: Mother and Daughter Reunited. Finally, after four generations, we are orphans no more. No more. Everything that could part us has been vanquished for-ever in this hug in the woods, where no one can see us and make it into just another story.

This is my happy ending, if there is any such thing when you consider that life always goes on!

You'd think Della and her daughter were runners, and may-be one day they will be. They'll do the 5K, then a half-marathon, then a whole one, and they won't care who's watching or why. It could be an all-woman marathon, or it might be men and women, adults and kids, who knows. The whole world will not be their judge, those weird men and women dressed in this or that, prancing about on their two legs, preening for each other and studying televi-sion to know what it is they need to buy in order to be happy. My girls are not of that world, and I'm really not sure how many girls ARE of that world. Or boys, for that matter.

That world is passing—not very gracefully, but definitely passing into something else, I hope something better. It's nice to be nice, but not when people use that as an excuse to stomp you. In the end, it's my hope that Della will NOT be nice to Tommy, as

NOT-nice as that sounds. It's a kindness, sometimes, to quit that charade of being nice. A kindness for all concerned.

I had the grace to die twice, under the moon, with dignity. Twice, I know now—once for myself, at 70, and once for my child self, who couldn't help leaving me. They dragged her away, kicking and screaming. This world is all chaos, all calamity, all self-consciousness as if somebody cared. God's rolling her eyes at the drama, I'm sure. But I am off topic. Of course Mama Otter, that little sweetie, leads my girls Della and Kierra straight to Uncle Ted, and of course it's clear with one glance that Ted needs a little more sleep, he's lying there like a dead slug. But this is not the place. Della is not so sure that her uncle is sober; she's not good at judging that, but what she can see for sure is that her daughter Kierra is at ease with him. Kierra toddles straight up to him and sits on his bony shoulder, which wakes him right away. He opens one eye. The rest of him does not move.

"Ted?"

No response from Ted, but his dog's doing her best to make up for that.

"Ted?" Della repeats. "Are you awake? Are you okay?"

"Ugh. Hey. Hey! Where's Kierra? Where'd she go?"

Della smiles. "She's right here. And there you are. You brought her to me. I guess I should thank you, but I haven't a clue what we're doing here, and I wish you hadn't fallen asleep and left her alone in the woods."

"We were both asleep. She must've woke up. I'm sorry." He hangs his head, but there's no point in this. Della can't be angry after everything that's happened, she's used up all of her "angry." He's family, and it seems that he cares a lot about Kierra and the whole situation.

"We're all doing the best we can," Della says, and she really means it. She's looking at her uncle with kindness. "I'm confused, not really sure what we're doing here. How did you get Kierra? What are you doing here?"

"I—she—well, I—She .... She brought you to me, Della."

"Who?"

"Granny..."

"Granny? Granny Elizabeth? Ted, it was the strangest thing, I followed this little otter—the one that's been sneaking into our house?—and I knew it would bring me to Kierra. I don't know how I knew that."

"No, not Grandma Elizabeth. Granny Colleen told you, not Elizabeth, an older one, an earlier grandma. You built your house practically on top of her cave, did you know that? You got her all worked up."

"What are you talking about? Are you okay? Did you hit your head?"

"I have never been better." Ted's offended. Now that he's feeling better, everyone should get with the program and understand, he's better, he's okay, he's got his head on straight. "I dreamed it. Then I looked it up. Then I met her. Don't you realize, your house is on the original family property, didn't your mother ever tell you that? Well, that's Cynthia, she never cared for genealogy."

"Nobody told me anything, except maybe that little river otter that guided me up this hill, and fool that I am, I just came, I followed orders from an otter and that was the best decision because here you both are, my Kierra, and my Uncle Ted."

"What time is it?"

"Ahh.. I don't know, Uncle Ted."

"Oh. Well. I have a phone, let's look." He fishes it out of his pocket, dimly aware that he's messed up somehow. "It's 8am, we're well into the morning already. See?"

She takes the phone, squints at it. "You've missed a couple of calls, it looks like."

"Oh, I saw that already. Just Cindy. Of course she'd be after me. I'll call her later, she might be asleep at this hour."

"Yeah, well, the police don't ever sleep, this is like the middle of the day for them. Uh... Ted?"

"Yeah?"

"I feel like they could follow you somehow."

"Follow me?" Ted replies, sitting up. Then he grabs his phone back from her, empties the battery. "Damn. Sorry about that. Guess I'm not as sober as I think."

"What's done is done."

"Well," he says. "Well." He tosses the phone into the air and catches it, twice. "I don't know what to do about this."

"Me either."

He gives Della a long look. He sighs loudly, then tosses his phone down the steep hill below the trail, then the battery, then the flimsy cover. "Maybe that'll buy us a little time, maybe not. I'm thinking they've got hounds, you know."

"Ted. What are you doing?"

"Hounds. Nosy dogs. Dogs that can sniff out whatever you tell 'm to."

"So you throw the phone down into the bushes?"

"It'll distract them."

"Anything else we could throw down there?" She's being sarcastic but he doesn't know it.

He's looking thoughtful. "It's hard to fool a hound. We can try walking in water again, like Jesus, that's what I started out with, but I ruined it by bringing my phone, and damn, my feet feel like a block of ice this morning."

"We should get moving, speaking of feet."

"Right."

Kierra's pulling on Della's arm now, looking distressed about something, and Ted says, "let's feed ourselves first, we got to eat."

"I have no food with me, Ted."

Ted grins, and whistles for Jeff the Dog. "We got that covered." He whistles again, and Jeff emerges from the woods, trots over to them and sits. Ted removes her doggie-backpack, empties out a dozen Baby Ruth bars onto the ground. Kierra stares at them with intense interest. "Tell you what," Ted says. "We each get one of these, and leave one bite for the nosy dogs, or the bears, whoever finds it first. We'll toss'm down there by my phone. Damn, I could've smeared some chocolate right on the phone. That'll throw'm off, maybe, just maybe, because any dog I ever met had a thing for chocolate. It's very distracting." Ted's lying, to make Della feel better, and who knows, maybe it'll work. The truth is, Ted knows next to nothing about scent hounds. No matter. I plan to help, to do whatever I can to stop any dogs or men or women, police or mundane hikers, whoever might come after my own people. We've come too far to fail now.

"Mama," Kierra says, pointing to the candy bars. She knows what they are and she wants one.

"See," Ted says, unwrapping one for Kierra, "the rest we'll take with us to eat later, and since they're all wrapped up tight in plastic, the dogs won't smell'm, and we'll have something to eat for a while yet."

He says to Kierra, "Just so you wash your hands, baby."

Kierra's chewing her Baby Ruth, smearing it on her face and fingers. I'm prodding Ms. Otter (who is disgusted by chocolate) to stay put, even though she longs for the big river. That's her element. Me, I've always been a mountain girl type of ghost. But she's got the French Broad in her mind's eye, the place she belongs, the place she meant to skitter off to more than a week ago, and we keep holding her up, she being a motherly type who understands what's going on, and what is at stake for us, and for her. If she can help me with my own river of women, make it run clear and true, then, Ms. Otter and her various friends, the salamander, the owl, the fish, the moss—they all will have a better chance to live as well. Like us, they all would like to continue. Mama Otter knows this better than anyone.

So once again, Ms. Otter agrees, she'll stay put, she'll distract the dogs if it's at all possible, she'll snack—or at least sniff—on some of that chocolate so the scent's on her nose and whiskers, and when they come she'll run like a bobcat, she'll forget her lopsided dyslexic land legs and run as if she's already in the water, and those dogs right after her, and the men thinking, "oh, they must've gone down to the river, he must have a boat," and at least half of them dividing off and following, diminishing their own forces, leaving the less intelligent ones up here on the trail. That's an advantage, a small one, but still an advantage for that little Kierra who must live. She must. I see it clear now, I understand what we're doing: We can't let them kill her by taking her away from her mother. I see that it is their chemicals that made the disease, and now they are trying to kill the disease with more chemicals. Wait on that, all of that! What about the mother? We are in the in-between already, the time has come to diminish the chemicals and return to the earth, resurrect the Mother Lovers who understand bark and petals and teas and cold water shock therapy.

Mush! Mooooshh!! I'm pushing them up the hill, blowing on them with my big chilly breath, huffing them upward, and Kierra knows to keep quiet, it's something Ted told her when nobody else was around, and I whispered it to her in her sleep, so now she's got her lips sealed. She keeps them pressed together, her cheeks puffed out with all the noise she wants to make. She's so much like the otter now, her little back humped into a curve as she presses herself against Ted's shoulders, riding in that homemade back-sling. After a while, she relaxes a bit, commences sucking her thumb. If she had whiskers, she'd be using them to check the air, to reassure herself that she is home, right here, right now.

Della walks behind so that she can keep her eyes on the love of her life. She's thinking about her mother, hoping Cynthia's not worried, but she knows she doesn't need to concern herself about Tommy, who looks after himself very well, thank you very much. It's clear now, out here in the woods: She loves him as you might love a distant relation, someone you shared a piece of your life with, or half a sandwich maybe… someone you've learned not to get too close to. Tommy is like a bear, beautiful in his way, but you get too close and he might eat you, or at the very least, he will most definitely bat at you, snarl, bite your ear off, even though you wear your friendliest smile and harbor your best intentions in your sincere heart. Admire the bear, admire him sincerely. Go ahead, love the bear as much as you like, just don't sleep with him, don't invite him into your home. Understand, Kierra? Della? Cynthia? You can love someone without trying to make them fit for your own sacred bed, and you can love someone without making yourself become what they are. You, Della, are a salamander if you only knew it. My darling girls! You're quiet, and flexible, and quick, and smart, and you need to be free. Give'em the slip. You can stand the cold—just think about last night, Della. You slept soundly after the sun set, no blanket, just you, curled up into you—and you've always liked the water.

You come from a line of women who worshipped the hemlock, and now, see, it's dying, that hemlock. Every last one, unless you pour a chemical on it, and that just can't be done, there's too many of them. When you hike through the forest, that's what you'll see, a graveyard of hemlocks. That's a sign for us to wake up for sure. I'm telling you.

Right there, where you met up with Ted? Healthy hemlocks were looking down on you, and my very bones supported your feet, my bones, feeding these trees, keeping these few hemlocks alive.

My bones, keeping you alive, Della. But you're still too much in the orphan trance to feel us all around you. Dimly, later on, you'll begin to notice that most of the hemlocks throughout these woods are dead skeletons, home for the food of the Pileated Woodpecker, tombstones memorializing the mountain forest that once was. I'm not blaming "human"-kind for this, when it was a little bug that did it and you can argue all day and all night how that little bug got to this continent, but who knows, it might have come here all on its own, that microscopic adelgid, and these trees may have been destined to fall. The adelgid wants to live, wants to expand, for its own sake, and anyone with life in them would understand that; but if the adelgid kills ALL the hemlocks, will the adelgid then die too? What I'm telling you is, watch what's around you. Listen to these dead trees, they are still speaking even if they are dead and not so pretty anymore. They are telling us something loud and clear. Nowadays you hear it in the rap-rap-rap of the woodpecker tapping her beak against the hemlock's tall corpse, tapping her beak like a nail into that wood, a beautiful sound, and you see it in all the powerful life going onward, moving forward, changing (from healthy green needles and flowing sap) to industrious insects and nests of baby birds and hibernating squirrels in the rotted, hollow places, the small caves and caverns that have manifested in what was once solid wood. One day the tree will fall, Della, and your own granddaughter will practice her balance by walking on it.

SIXTEEN

Ms. Otter wobbles down the side of the mountain, a piece of Baby Ruth held distastefully in her teeth. We journey upward and onward, me the ghost, Ted with Kierra in her sling clinging to his neck, Della and Jeff the Dog leading the way. As we first start out, the little girl, like her mother, is frightened but determined, you can see it in the tilt of her head. Looking upward and forward. Then she sleeps. Life moves on. The day's lifting itself into warmth and silence but Ted's footsteps are heavy and Della's downright stomping, smashing that silence and churning up heat. We go like this all day long, without stopping, and there's no way I'm turning back to check on anybody else—the police, Lawrence and Maggie, Cynthia, even Cynthia's mother Amy Ellen Elizabeth (I couldn't check on her if I tried—she's crossed through my world and gone on ahead of me). I've left them all behind and you know, they can feel it. It's a difference that's hard to describe, but you feel it when someone's left you alone, ask any orphan. That's okay, it's meant to be, I am called onward now. Really, I don't miss it, that energy I once had to be in several places at once, or to fly from one loved one to another, peeking into this window, slipping under that door. My focus is narrowing as I grow older and wiser. It's all about Kierra now.

It's a day, a night, and another day of walking. It's a miracle they haven't caught up to us. We pass many dead hemlocks and burgeoning rhododendrons much taller than Ted, beautiful tangled things just beginning to bud, though it seems off season, and above us, twice, a red-tailed hawk. As we approach Ol' Granny's house, which is tucked high up behind a rock outcropping and out of sight of any path or road above or below it, we encounter a she-bear. She's not close—well, she's close enough—and I don't see any cubs for her to get all riled up about. In fact, she's quite calm. She's standing on two feet, sniffing the air, watching us, and I can tell by looking at her that she won't move until we've passed. Bears can be stubborn like that, knowing they're bigger than we are, and just because they've spent their entire life on one mountain they think it's theirs. Ted puts his finger on his lips, gesturing for everyone to be quiet and ignore the bear. He ducks under a wild dogwood and peaks around a five-foot chunk of quartz, then disappears with Kierra still on his back. She whimpers for no apparent reason. Della hurries to catch up, but I'm feeling strangely weak and slow. They won't go far now—we're in a steep place here, not much further forward left for us to go before we all have to circle back. I know there's a cliff, but I don't know how I know.

The Knowing—it's getting stronger.

What's this? I can smell the ocean from here. We're centuries away from that. But it's okay, I suppose. I thought I would hate it, but it's a clean, salty smell, and it seems as if it would discuss something with me, in a friendly way, and now I'm remembering again what I want to forget—that a grandmother before me crossed the ocean once, just once, she birthed a wee child, and that voyage gifted her with an awakening, a long-sought escape—and a terrible death as well. Did she die, or was it her baby? Somehow, someone ended up alone in the New World, found herself in a large and dangerous land, alone. And then, there was the "getting on with it" that people do, over and over again. We get on with it. We are told to forget the particulars, so said the patriarchs.

○

I'm knowing this, and somehow it gives me strength to turn the corner and continue forward, following my compatriots to Ol' Granny's cabin, which is more cavern than cabin. Three sides of it are rock, a natural cave in the side of Bear Cub Mountain, while the fourth side—overlooking the valley—is a mass of windows, an odd collection of mismatched glass panes collected from abandoned houses and trash piles, held together in some places with wood and in other places, rock and concrete. Della and Ted are standing just outside the door, scanning the view. A white pool of fog covers the bottomland so thick, that for a moment I think it might be a lake down there. I blink at it, then blink at my friends. My people have turned, now, to knock on the thin wooden door. When there's no answer, they step inside. Ted's healer friend, "Ol' Granny," is sitting up in her bed, a sketch pad in her lap, a chunk of charcoal in her left hand. She's wearing, incongruously, a huge diamond on her left ring finger, must be a carat, maybe two. Jeff the Dog jumps onto the bed, smells something she doesn't like, jumps back down, patters over to the doorway and lies down in the threshold, her little head on her front leg, her eyes open, watching, waiting for the next thing, while the fragile door swings back and forth on its hinges, skreeking rhythmically as if counting out the endless hours.

Still holding the charcoal, Ol' Granny slowly extends her left hand in what looks to be a little wave, or a beckoning. When Ted turns to show her the little girl on his back, Ol' Granny smiles big, her whole face crinkling up like a wadded-up paper bag—at which Kierra recoils and flings her arms out to her mother, who quickly takes her out of the sling on Ted's back and holds her up high against her chest, but it's not high enough, Kierra's still scrambling as if she would climb her mother like a tree. I have to laugh, a sound like a laughing gull, and sure enough, there she is, a seagull coasting past the windows. We are near the ocean? No. I am near the ocean, they are not. Something is happening to me, I am in two places at once. One of my feet stands in sand, the other on rock.

Ted bends over to give Ol' Granny a hug; he presses his hand to her cheek and says, "Hey there, Granny. It's been a long time, hasn't it?"

She nods.

"You've lost weight. I've missed you."

She blinks back, as if to reply the same.

"We're in a hurry."

Granny frowns her disapproval.

"I'm sorry, but we're in a hurry, I know you don't like to be hurried, life is too short, I know. But we're in a hurry, so I'll tell you what we've come for. I've brought this little girl to meet you, she's been sick. Her name is Kierra. They started her on a medicine for her cancer but they say the odds aren't good for the medicine to save her. It will only prolong her life. Right, Della?"

"That's how I understood it." Della steps forward; Kierra climbs a little higher. Della's unhappy with Ted for saying this in front of Kierra; who knows how much the girl understands? But it's too late, he's already said it. "Is there anything you can do to help us?" Della asks. "We're sorry to come in on you like this—"

The old lady interrupts by shaking her head vigorously.

"What?" Della looks at Ted.

Ted says, "She doesn't talk."

"Oh."

Granny smiles and nods. She returns to her sketch pad, turns the tablet to a fresh, blank page, and, very quickly, with her left hand, she creates a picture of Kierra, then lifts the paper up, awkwardly, with just her left hand, showing it to them all. Kierra relaxes an inch, stares at the picture. Then points, wanting it.

"She hasn't talked in years," Ted says.

"You didn't tell me that," Della whispers back, covering her mouth, hoping the old lady is as deaf as she is dumb. "She doesn't talk? How can she help us?"

"Put Kierra down on the bed. You'll see."

Kierra's already shaking her head. NO.

"This is not going to work," says Della. But I can see what needs to happen, it's good I am here, because I can talk to the little girl, I can whisper to her to look at that!, and she looks, and she sees all the colors in a small woven basket on Granny's bedside table, crayons and pastels and colored pencils. Now, she's thinking about it. There's a shift that Della can feel in her daughter's little body.

"Give her a minute," Della says, suddenly weak in the knees as it begins to occur to her—this is ludicrous. She's going to lose her child over this. Her daughter needs medical care, not a lunatic old lady who lives in her bed, on a rock ledge, with a basket of crayons for visitors.

But she has more than crayons. Granny points to a cabinet over a small ceramic basin, and Ted obediently goes to open it— inside, a loaf of bread wrapped in wax paper, unspoiled, and beside that a jar of almond butter, some bags of rice and some bags of dried beans, a jar of some type of juice, and canned jams. "Della?" he says, "Set Kierra down there on the bed, and come help make lunch, can you?"

"Should we?" Della whispers. "Aren't those her groceries?"

"She wants to share. It always gets refilled. She has friends."

"Sure," Della says in a loud, almost-normal voice. "I can help make us all some lunch. Here, you sit here, honey," and with the hope of food in her tummy (she saw the almond butter and she thinks it is peanut butter), Kierra complies, and soon she's snuggled next to Ol' Granny in spite of the stink. She's coloring and scribbling, smearing the paper in that abstract style of the two-year-old. Kierra does not seem to be feeling sick, despite the long trek, and Della, glancing over her shoulder to look at Kierra every thirty seconds or so, is aware of this change. She's wondering if she should take her daughter back to the real doctors, as it appears the medicine might actually be helping her.

"It's not," Ted whispers, reading her thoughts.

"What?" Della whispers back.

"That prescription they started her on. It's not helping, believe me. You think we need to get Kierra back to the doctors, don't you? I'll tell you, that chemical stuff isn't helping. We used lots of chemicals in 'Nam, and all I know is, they ruin life, chemicals kill little girls and a lot of other things too. This medicine, it's just another poison. What's helping Kierra is love, Della. It's love, here. Kierra feels it. She knows you hiked up through the woods alone and at night, in the scary dark, somehow she knows that, she knows you slept under the open sky, she knows you would do anything to find her. Children know stuff. They know when they're loved or not loved. She's already figured out that she doesn't have to be afraid of Ol' Granny, because Ol' Granny sees into your heart and loves you right there in the middle of your heart, and that's all she sees and that's all she does. She loves. Doesn't matter how sick you might be, she sees your heart. Kierra's responding to that."

"How would you know... you don't have kids...." He doesn't have a wife either, or any true friends, but Della doesn't want to point that out, it seems cruel.

"I just know. I've seen it before. That girl," he gulps, choking on his words, "I have to tell you. The one we killed... I killed, I believe it was my shot, not on purpose, and it was probably a gift because that village got napalmed right afterwards. But her eyes, you could see it in her eyes, she knew what was happening, and she was smarter than all of us, she was already on the road to forgiveness, I could see all of that in her eyes."

"Maybe, Ted. Maybe we can talk to each other like that, without words, is that what you mean?"

"I don't think so. I think I'm talking about love, actually, just love. Well I've been asking her forgiveness all my life but the only time I felt it was that second before she... died, you know?" He stops, wipes his forehead with the back of his hand. There's a blush coming up his neck. "I was holding her, and I felt her forgiving me in advance, she knew she was dying. But how could she forgive me? That doesn't make any sense, unless you think in terms of love, some big love that crosses war zones. I felt it then. And now I can't get it back, I think it was just... wishful thinking on my part, or something like that. I don't deserve to be forgiven. I guess I don't want it, really. The only way I could accept her forgiveness would be if I could make her come back to life. I owe her that. It was my fault she died."

Della's watching Ted's face, wondering if he's sincere or holding a little pity party for himself. He's so articulate, so smart. She decides it's the former, it's sincerity, because he hasn't had a drink in four days to the best of her knowledge, and there's a different kind of look in his eyes—clarity, perhaps. Determination, maybe. Love? He's wanting to grow up, that's what it is. He's staring at the floor, though, and shame's pouring out through his skin, pooling on the floor beneath him, right where he's staring, sticking to his shoes, holding him from moving. It's a sort of bluish-purple color, the color of the bulging veins on Ol' Granny's hands.

Della inhales and says, "That's because you need to forgive yourself, Ted. It's not her forgiveness anymore. Forgive yourself." She sighs, chews her lip. For a moment, there's a thoughtful, unfocused look in her little green eyes. Then she continues, "That's an old saw, I know, but it's true. That girl you killed, she's gone on. You can't change it."

Ted's working his jaw and I'm glad there's no alcohol up here in Ol' Granny's cupboards.

"I forgive you, Ted. I'm a mother, and I forgive you."

He looks up.

Me, I'm dumbstruck, this is a wisdom that orphans like my Della don't often exhibit. Maybe the generations are learning, after all. She's getting real close to her own freedom.

Della continues, "I followed that otter up to the trail, Ted, I went on my intuition until I saw you there with Kierra, and then I believed, I got some hope in me, so I followed you on up the trail to this God-forsaken place." She smiles at herself. "Okay, maybe not God-forsaken. But to me, it seems like the otter trusted you, led me to you."

"You want to go back." Ted shifts his weight, sticks his hands in his pockets.

"I do, Ted."

He still can't move. "I want to go back. I want to go back to Viet Nam."

"Look," says Della, "There's a lot of unfinished business that is no longer your business. We did enough over there, we have to leave them alone."

"I need to make amends."

"Start here. Be here with me. Now."

Ted looks up, blinks at his niece. "She... you...."

"I'm tired, Uncle Ted. I'm worried about Kierra. I want to get out of here."

"Yes. Yes, I understand." For a moment he's bright red, and then just as fast the blush is gone; I can tell something has left him, it's like a bird just flew out of his chest.

"What can we do about this nice lady here? Who takes care of Ol' Granny?"

"She..." He's remembering something.

Della's impatient. "I asked, who takes care of Ol' Granny? We can't just leave her here by herself."

"You're right. Um. Lawrence, actually, last time I knew of it. Maggie and Lawrence have known her forever. They—" Ted squints. It's hitting him like a hammer, I can see it coming down against his eyes, the realization that Lawrence knows exactly where Ted has taken Kierra. He knows where we are.

"They ... what?"

Ted shakes his head, hard. "Never mind. Let's just eat, and let Kierra sit with Granny, let her soak up the blessing, and then we'll head out."

"Soak up the blessing? Ted? I thought she was some kind of doctor, you know, herbs and such."

"We shouldn't stay here too long, you're exactly right about that. We'll have to be heading out again. Soon."

"Somebody needs to bless Ol' Granny and get HER out of here—this is no place for an old lady!"

"That's right, Della, just a blessing from Granny will do, and... and, whatever kind of tea she prepares, Kierra should drink it. Then we'll go."

"But—"

"We'll, ah, we'll keep hiking, we will hike over to... ah, over to... the Mountain-to-Sea Trail? Yes, and that'll get us to the ocean eventually. Then we'll get her to a good doctor, whoever you want, I'll pay. We won't look back." He's in the mood for a drink, remembering the bars in Wilmington, just two hours from Ft. Bragg, wanting out of this straight-jacket house, squeezed between all these women.

"Ted, we can't last that long. We have one candy bar left, and we can't rob Granny's pantry."

"Yes, you can." It's Granny speaking, and that even makes ME jump, and me a ghost, but Ted's more upset than I am. His face is white as mine and he's frozen, staring at her.

"Jesus," she says.

"What?" Ted stammers.

"Take all of it," Ol' Granny says. "Jesus, the living Christ."

"Granny? Is that you?" Ted walks to her bedside, leans over her, his hand on her arm. "Are you talking?"

Granny nods. "I am not.... making tea today. Listen, dear... ones.... I have ... only... three ... words... left."

He sees it now, she's had a stroke of some sort, she's not moving her legs or her right arm, and all at once he can smell it, the ripe, invading smell of death.

".....TAKE.... IT.... ALL...."

She smiles, blinks at Ted, and lifts her left hand to pet Kierra's head the way old people pet children. As she rests her hand atop that soft silk, she stops, just like that, she stops, her diamond ring glimmering up at them like creek water sparkling in the sun.

TAKE IT ALL, that's what she said.

Kierra just goes on drawing, unaware of the strength of the blessing flowing down upon her head, unaware that Ol' Granny is officially dead. That old hand will remain warm for a long time.

O

Ol' Granny won't leave right away, anyone knows that. She stays even longer because she sees me clearer than I can see myself, which feels so good, and we mingle, compare notes about the physical world and the weightless plane of existence, and she'd like a couple of pointers though she is already beginning to remember this place from another time. She knows she was supposed to wait for us up here on the mountain, and she's happy we came. A hundred and eight years is long enough to live. And she's telling me that she sees Kierra grown up, that our Kierra will survive and thrive and in fact will go to some kind of medical school. But for now—our little Kierra—for life to go on she needs to go back. She needs the doctors and the Mother Lovers, her family and our prayers, one alone will not help, in any direction. She needs all of it. That's the message Ol' Granny blesses me with, she entrusts me with, to pass along, somehow, to my people. Ol' Granny trusts me not to be a pest of the living, not to linger too much longer—she knows about the part of me that was hoping for someone to join me, to cross that ocean with me. I must stop waiting, she tells me. Orphan that I am, I will have to make that final journey alone.

As for Ol' Granny, the moon will be full tonight, as full as a crystal ball. She'll be on her way, she intends to pass through and the conditions are right, exactly, wonderfully, perfectly right, and that is a rare thing indeed. She knows she's fulfilled every last detail of her work here. She's especially pleased by that final blessing of Kierra, that last oomph of LIFE flowing through her, flowing smooth and hot out through the palm of her hand and onto Kierra's head like a warm knit cap. For all Kierra's life that blessing will be sinking in, nourishing her just like my bones fed those hemlocks and kept them alive.

Ol' Granny Apple is ready, so very ready, to go.

Ted's taking the lavender diamond ring. "It's okay, we're related," Ted mumbles as he slips it off her warm, knotty finger. "We're all related."

Suddenly I can't see her, and just as suddenly, I know who she is: George Bright Apple's mother. She's here still—the moon's not up—but I can't see her, and that's the last she'll speak to me. Kierra, in this same moment, startles and looks at Ol' Granny, stares into Ol' Granny's unseeing eyes; Kierra takes it in, this absolute absence of life, then she looks at her mother, both of them with question marks in their eyes, regarding each other now with love, a deep love made more real by this death thing happening in the same room with them. Della scoops Kierra up into her arms. Kierra looks from her mother's face, to the ceiling, and back to her mother—and smiles an angelic smile that seems to mirror the happiness of Ol' Granny right at this very moment in space and time, which is timeless, as you'll find out in your own time.

SEVENTEEN

As for Ted, he stuffs that ring into Della's palm. He closes her fingers around it, and now he's packing up. She's standing there staring at the ring for the longest time with him bustling around her, until she says "No, I can't take this," and Ted says, "Really, you can, hon." Finally she tiptoes over to the bedside and plants the ring back into Ol' Granny's hand, but it won't stay there, it just slides down onto the sheets. She picks it up again.

"See? She wants you to have it, Della."

As for me, I'm trying to figure out how to get them to turn around, NOT to trod on down to the ocean, the closest beach being CHARLESTON, and that's a five hour DRIVE from here. They can't hitch-hike, due to the Amber alert.

And the hounds are loose. Just as I can smell the ocean many days ahead of us, I can smell the hounds coming up behind us, much closer than that. There are two hounds in the pack that are particularly well trained, running out front of the others. I can smell their joy! Scott and Mattie are shelter dogs, but for them the past is dead, lucky beings. In the last two days they've smelled milk chocolate with peanuts, they've scrambled through an icy creek, and they've chased the otter. Contrary to being broken by their puppyhood, they are tough, and they know what they like to do: Smell and chase. That's what they like: the smell, the chase. Unbroken muses, beautiful mutts. They've caught our scent.

"Run!" I scream to Ted, and to my dismay he can barely hear me. He just slightly tilts his head, as if there's a tickle in his ear, then he seems to think a minute.

"Run!" Ted yells, suddenly, making Della jump and Kierra cry. Jeff the Dog leaps out the door and sets out ahead of them, running back down the trail in the direction they came from. "Not that way!" Ted yells to Jeff the Dog, who circles 'round, meeting back up with her people, bumping into Ted's shins at the fork in the path above Ol' Granny's cave. But that same bear they met on their way in has lumbered onto the path and is sitting upright picking berries. The bear just stares at them, unmoving. On one side of the trail, a drop-off. On the other side, a rhododendron hell so thick that it's impassable, and if they were to try it, and get stuck, that bear could just ramble on down and have a NICE snack on all three of them. They're frozen there, until Jeff the Dog springs forward and commences barking with all the gusto a 30-pound mutt can muster.

The bear's unmoved. Must be good berries. I could try going into her body, like my earlier collaboration with Ms. Otter, but this bear is clearly not interested. There's nothing to do, but back up. Now we are trapped between two bases, the ocean and the family cabin. Run forward? Run back? Ol' Granny's gone, so it's up to me now, and the hounds… I hear'm barking. Then Della can hear them, she hears those hounds pounding up the mountain, then Ted hears them, and they're off on a run, into the rhododendron, kicking their way through, trying to make a wide detour around the bear, Kierra crying again (out of fear or confusion, I don't know), Della irritably shushing her. That Della, she's had almost all she can take.

The bear, just as I thought, she's noticed the commotion, she's cocking her head at the sound of humans bumbling through dead branches, and she's on her feet now, rumbling down the hill toward them, and Ted can only hear my voice once, only ONCE in all this racket. I have a queasy feeling that some part of my spirit has taken off with Ol' Granny, called it quits, and I am weaker and smaller than ever—the moment Ted removed her ring, that's when I felt it. With that diamond now in Della's pocket, I am already less needed—she's got a down payment on Kierra's cancer treatment, if she keeps that ring. I guess we'll see.

"Ted! Bear! Go back!" My last words?

He only hears "Back!" ever so faintly, but he stops, looks up, and goes eye-to-eye with the bear, not 10 yards away.

"Back!" he yells, grabbing Kierra from Della, slashing a pathway back down through the rhododendron, back to Ol' Granny's place. They'll be cornered there, but at least they can shut the door on the bear. I'm pushing them hard as I can, careful not to cause them to fall or stumble over that cliff-side of the trail, and they're going to make it, they're going to… almost… and then I see I'm going to have to turn and stop that bear myself, somehow, even if it kills me, even if it sends me who-knows-where. I stand my ground, and suddenly, Runner's with me—only for a second—there she is, my original mother, her front feet planted, guarding me. Bear stops. Ted pushes Kierra and Della into the house, then scoops up Jeff the Dog, slams the door behind them all. He turns and watches through the crack that runs down the middle of the door. He can't see me, of course; all he can see is that enormous black bear standing before him, inches from that door. She must be six feet tall. Her black fur glistens in the afternoon sun as she rocks back and forth in a little dance of nonchalance, or self-soothing, her paws waving lazily in the air. Then she seems to hear something new… it's those hounds… and she's off, skittering away to some hiding place of her own, taking the hounds with her, the hounds on her heels, happy, barking, fierce, confident, their human handlers distracted and astounded that they've come upon a bear. Perhaps those hounds are not so smart, or not so wise—or maybe they're our angels after all. Their youth with all that ripe DNA, those centuries of breeding, that programming altogether turns their heads toward the heady scent of BEAR, a more wonderful prize than anything else, a target-scent trained into their ancestors over the past two hundred years and more. After all, it was their mother's and their mother's mother's proud job to smell out the bear, the bear being a winter's feast, as well as two if not three winter coats for the offspring of pioneering humans. The bear is fat, sustenance, blanket, second skin, life.

○

There's a sincere clattering of paws against stone, the small sound of two earnest voices debating where the trail leads, and they're missing this hiding spot completely, following the hounds, going off to the left where the path forks, leaving Ol' Granny's territory forever for lower ground and fruitlessness. I suspect Ol' Granny herself had something to do with this, not wanting her bones disturbed at this critical moment—it could interfere with her journey if they came in and bungled with her body. Me, my ghostly self? I'm in the in-between again, shut out from the cabin, diminished even further by the bear. The wind is harsh up here. Maybe that's why I feel so thin and floppy, pushed about, smoky, sad. For the first time, a hint of jealousy—envy that Ol' Granny's found herself worthy to go on to the big place, where there's music and love and light, and here I still swim in circles, still embracing this old world like it's my own big old baby. I'm unfinished, frozen, looking for something that someone else lost so I can go on, yes that's it, something that someone else lost. What is it? For heaven's sake. I know what it is.

Footsteps.

Kierra sits on the floor, coloring again. Ol' Granny lies undisturbed, staring without seeing, her mouth open. Ted and Della stand by the door, their ears perked up, listening for any sound, any sound at all besides the swirling, incessant wind, which is actually me. Ted and Della can't hear me anymore, I know that, unless they can understand what the wind is saying. I tried to tell them about the footsteps, but they couldn't understand. It's an emptiness, a loneliness. Only wind and more wind. What would they do, anyway, if they could hear my instructions? What would I tell them to do? This is a dead-end. I'm losing my sense of what's going on, and there's a flash of Elizabeth, she tells me she feels the same way, and I feel her presence leaning into me, then it's gone. I remember her long-ago loss of George. Then Thomas Miller, my own one love, he's kissing my ear, and gone, too, and I'm alone with the footsteps, growing louder, closer. Finally, Della hears them too. She hears them before Ted, her hearing being better than his. She grabs his arm, gives him a shake. He nods his head, uncomprehending.

"Someone's coming. I hear them."

He presses his ear against the crack in the door. Nothing. He looks at her, questioning, then he hears it. Yes. Footsteps.... And a song. Yes, a song. "I am solid as a mountain... I am firm as the earth... I am blooming like a flower... I am fresh as the dew... I am free, I am free, I am free...."

"Oh God," says Ted. It's Lawrence. He's in good shape, singing while he hikes uphill, not even breathless. Of course, he hasn't been running from the law for three days, though I doubt he slept much. Then, barking. Oh dear God. More bounty hunters, more hounds. There are two of them, two ferocious dogs, and together they rush at the door, one of them slamming into it. But they're not hounds. It's Sheba, a black lab, along with Thaddeus, the big old yellow fellow belonging to Lawrence, both of them barking because they've sniffed Jeff, or maybe the bear, who knows, but they're not hunters, they're not hounds, they just happen to have come in the right direction, full tilt, and there's nothing to do but open the door. Lawrence pushes past the dogs and steps inside, followed by his wife Maggie, who puts her foot out and closes the door on their dogs with an ease that suggests they've been up here many, many times before.

"Your daughter's foster parents," Ted says softly, and Kierra looks up, such a smart little thing. "Della, this is it. Sorry."

Della steps back. She steps back from everything, feeling very small. She wants to pick Kierra up, but she knows that would only distress her daughter, who seems content, a crayon dangling in her hand. If her daughter cries for any reason, they'll suspect abuse. There's still a charcoal pencil dangling in Ol' Granny's hand and the two of them—Kierra and Granny—look alike, for a moment, like the beginning point and the ending point of the same being, two sides of one collectible coin.

A big bark-fest has begun, all dogs yakking and jerking their heads in the air, one inside, two outside, so Ted opens the door, why not. Jeff zips out, then a circle of butt sniffing and tail wagging before they're all three gone, bounding up the hill and clattering in circles on top of Ol' Granny's cavern, then no sound at all. They could be galloping off to alert the other dogs, but who cares anymore, there's nothing left to be done. I've settled my cloaky self down across Kierra's shoulders for my own comfort as much as hers. She's my girl. There is something about this child's still peacefulness, I don't feel as if I'm mooching, it doesn't quite come from her. She's still, and calm, as she leans back over her paper and continues to scribble. I'm feeling my departure coming soon, too soon. I want to see this little one grow up, she'll stand tall, I know it. She won't use plastic bags, and she'll have herself a little garden, I'm sure of it. She's got my eyes, this one.

"I knew you'd come," Ted says.

"I knew I'd find you here," Lawrence replies. Then he sees Della hiding behind the door, and extends his hand, "I'm Lawrence Castleman," he says. "Pleased to meet you."

"Same," Della mumbles, shaking his warm hand, but trembling as she says, "This is MY daughter Kierra, but I guess you've met." She didn't mean to sound like that but that's how it came out. "Sorry," she says.

"Yes, we kept Kierra for a night. Maggie, meet Della, Kierra's mom."

Suddenly the cabin is warm with bodies, people shaking hands, introducing each other again. Maggie prefers to hug, so that starts off a round of hugs. When that's finished Lawrence sits down on Ol' Granny's bed and rests a hand on her knee. "I see that our Old Granny Apple has moved on at last," he says.

"Just now," says Ted.

"She died right in front of us," Della explains. "She seemed happy, like she was so glad to see us, and then it seemed like... like she was ready to go, just waiting for us to arrive. Do you think... do you think it will traumatize Kierra?" She wants to sound concerned in the proper way, though it seems to her that death is a natural thing and if it happens, it happens. Kierra didn't seem that upset. But Della is no longer the authority—the foster parents have the power, the expertise, the final say. She says all that too, in her expression, fighting back tears.

Lawrence shrugs. Instead of answering her question, he asks, "Are you okay?" For one thing, he hates that word, trauma. Also, he's familiar with that sort of question from biological parents, who want you to think they are good, that they know things. I want to tell Lawrence that yes, Della IS good, she knows A LOT, and she should have her child back; the only trauma was that they took the child from her.

"I suppose," Della answers. "As okay as I can be, under the circumstances."

"I figured Ted would be here," Lawrence continues. "But I'll confess I'm surprised to see YOU. They've been trying to find you since yesterday, to let you know your daughter was kidnapped. The thing is, they were getting ready to release her back to you. There was no sign of any wrongdoing until now."

"I know, I know. I made a huge mistake."

"What were you thinking?" Lawrence asks.

"Nothing," says Ted. "She wasn't thinking nothing. She was walking up into the woods to think everything over and she run into me. I was hiking up to the cabin. Her only mistake was to listen to me, I said I knew someone up here that could help Kierra get better, and that's the main thing. This little one has got cancer. I just wanted to take the little girl away from the people that can hurt her, I.E. THE USA GOVERNMENT. I have first-hand experience about that. How can a little girl come through cancer without her mother there holding onto her? Answer that. And then if you can answer that, tell me, what's worse, dying of cancer, or losing your mother? Aren't they about the same? Why cause both of those things to happen to an innocent little child in one day? Two deaths! Who gives them the right to make things worse?"

"Good question, Ted, but here's the issue at hand—they were releasing the child. It was a mistake to take her."

Maggie says, "They didn't know, Lawrence."

"Della," says Lawrence, "What needs to happen now?"

"Well. We need to get off the mountain, and I would love to bring Kierra home. She should follow up with her doctors, and I want to take some time off so I can just hold her. I just want to hold her."

"Good, then, you won't mind my telling you. You've lost your job—because you went AWOL without calling in. Tommy's been interviewed. He says if you and Ted took off with the baby—and he guessed right about that—that's grounds for divorce. So I expect he'll be filing for divorce, filing for custody."

"Bullshit," says Ted, rubbing his throat. "He don't mean that."

"Could be," says Maggie, "But he can do that if he wants to, and there's at least one judge I know that likes to give kids to their dads, either that or more often he splits them in half, fifty-fifty. Spiteful fellow."

"Sometimes that works out," says Lawrence, and Maggie gives him a look that says everything she's ever said on that subject, while Della seems about to faint. "Don't worry," Lawrence continues, "We can put everything back the way it was, if Ted can keep a promise."

"I don't want everything back—" Della starts, then stops herself.

"Don't what? Listen, Della..." Lawrence glances at Maggie, who nods solemnly, which terrifies Della. "...Sit down and let me tell you what I know. You'll be fine, Della. You don't need to worry about your job right now."

"I have to make a living."

"Would you mind to sit down?"

She sits, slowly, reluctantly.

"Della, everybody needs to find their calling. You're not going to lose your daughter. Being a mother is part of your calling, a big part. But you are sitting on another part of your own calling and you don't even know it." He pauses, as if he can't quite decide on the words. Ted's mouth is moving like he wants to say it, whatever it is.

"My calling?" Della asks. She looks at Ted, who looks up at the ceiling.

"I'll just tell you," Lawrence continues. " You're, well, you're Granny Apple's niece. Well, great-niece or great-great-niece. On your mother's side, you see, going back to... let's see, I had it. Your great-great-grandmother Colleen Nicholson had a twin brother, but they were raised apart. If these things... these recent events... hadn't happened, we might not ever have put that together." A pause. "I try to track the family when I take in a foster kid. Sometimes you can find family to place them with."

Another pause.

"That's why she told us to take it all," Ted says, interrupting the silence. "Granny said 'TAKE IT ALL' right before she died. Della thought she meant the food, but I knew. I just knew it."

"Sh," says Maggie.

"What are you saying?" Della asks. I'm right close to her cheek listening to this.

"This is your mountain, Della."

Della would faint—if she believed him. This is going to take some time, and she can't think of what to say. She stands up, stretches, walks over to the windows.

"Della?" Lawrence says softly. "When we get back down the mountain, I'll show you, in black and white. Apparently she knew about you, but she had her peculiar ways. I'm not surprised she never contacted you. She was a very private person."

Della nods without turning from the windows. She's watching a flock of white seagulls pass, circle, pass again.

"Ted, I know you can keep a promise," Lawrence says. "One very important promise." His bushy eyebrows raised, Lawrence is staring at Ted like a bossy mother. You can actually see the whites of his eyes.

"I'll try."

"Not good enough. One promise, Ted."

"Okay, you've got me, I'll do it."

"I don't—" Della starts again. "I want to say—"

"Promise you won't do this again," Lawrence says. "No more kidnapping."

"Oh, that? That I can do, no problem." Ted replies. "I was hasty. I was only a couple days off whiskey. If I had it to do over, I wouldn't do it now. Absolutely not."

"Thing is, you might get drunk again and come over to my house, Ted. You might forget. You might black out. They'll give Kierra back to us for now, but not if you're on the loose. Nobody will believe you if you say you're sorry, you'll never do it again. You might do it again. Whether or not that's true, people will think you might. We can't have that."

"I know, I know."

"So what do you suggest. What're we going to do?" Lawrence asks. "I can believe your promise. In fact, I DO believe you, but I'm probably the only one, west of Raleigh."

"Send him to detox," says Della. "He'll go. Won't you, Ted."

"We can't take him to detox," Maggie says, "unless he's intoxicated."

"I can do that," says Ted, and I'm thinking he must be joking but he's not, his eyes are dead serious. Then he laughs. "I can do that," he repeats, and yes, he really means it, bad as it sounds. Everybody can see that. "I'll even go to those meetings. 'God grant me the serenity to accept the people I cannot change, the courage to change the one I can, and the wisdom to know it's me.'"

"Okay then, okay then," Lawrence is saying, "let's give this some thought...." But I am fading out, fainting, even though I would love to hear what's up their sleeves as they plot how to set this up, how to get Ted drunk but not too drunk, how to finesse him into detox instead of jail, but that's a stiff order, how to make it look okay for Della, as if she had nothing to do with anything, and I can almost hear it, oh yes, here it comes in stronger, my Della confiding something, something about how maybe she doesn't want to go back to Tommy, even if he does change his mind about the divorce, and we know he will. Maybe she and her mother Cynthia could find a place, and there's that Christian woman, Monica Davidson, that first-shift waitress who befriended Della. She takes an interest. They might just stay with Monica until Della knows what she wants, and until the phone calls from Tommy (with all his threats and promises) die down, so that she can find out whether they can really talk to each other and work things out, or not.

"No, Della!" That's me talking, banging my head against the wall actually, because she's moving back into the dense world, the world of what to say next and where to live and what to feed Kierra, the world where she can't hear me. No, I'm saying, don't go to Monica Davidson, try that other girl Rachel instead, the one who works second shift. Rachel's what I call a Red Letter Christian.

"Red Letters," Ted mumbles. He's still hearing me, after all, but this is the last time, those are my last words. He's almost thinking about it, those words highlighted in red, what's it called, a red letter Bible?—but then it's lost to a wind that just won't quit.

"What?" Della asks.

"I don't know, what did I just say?"

"You read a letter?" Della's smiling with a sort of relief, a sort of wonderment. She owns a mountain?

"What were we talking about?"

"Programs, Uncle Ted. We don't know any other way to do this. You're going to have to turn yourself in, and hope that we can advocate for you to get into a program, not jail. I'll supply the reading materials. You really liked those books by that Vietnamese monk with the funny name. You said his books could've been written by Jesus, if you just go by what Jesus said and not all those commentaries."

"I'd forgotten. Yeah. Yeah, Lawrence, you turned me on to that, the Vietnamese Jesus. Now you're going to turn me in."

Lawrence laughs out loud. "You bet I am," he grins.

EIGHTEEN

And I'm leaving them like that. I can't stick around for Kierra's birthday, but I have Ol' Granny's promise: With the doctors and the Mother Lovers putting their heads together, my Kierra will triumph and become some sort of doctor herself one day, for people, for animals, for the environment, we don't know yet. I see Della leaving Tommy, at least long enough to get her strength back, living with her mother of all people, and one day Uncle Ted gets free after serving time both in jail and in rehabilitation, he's got himself back, and he comes on home to help out. A few years after that maybe Tommy himself, Kierra's father, having thought it over, will step back into the picture giving a little something of himself to his grown daughter. You never know what tomorrow may bring. I also see Ted learning to meditate, with Jeff the Dog (arthritic but loyal) meditating beside him, and I see Lawrence and Maggie taking in another child to care for, and then another, and Maggie a mother to Della, and to Kierra, when they need her. I feel myself drifting, too tired to resist, knowing I'm done, I'm done with my work.

For every blunder, there was a gift. For every attempt to help, there was some blunder. It all balanced out in the long run, even though it's still not perfect and never will be. I want to follow Ol' Granny, and she's telling me I can, I hear her kind motherly voice telling me to let it go, it's enough, I am enough. Though I am telling you, there isn't much to let go of, I'm not much these days. I'm the stringiest wisp of a wisp, the tiniest, most tense little cord of sinewy self that used to be, that wants to fly once more, just one time all the way around the planet. If only the ocean did not scare me so much, I would embrace the whole earth.

I'm floating on bird wing, on the back of a solitary crow—who knows, it might be the one I saw fly out of Ted's chest. The crow passes through a wisp of cloud and sheds me there. I lose a little more of me to the cloud, but I'm still here, I'm still here. Alone, I'm flowing down the side of the last steep mountain, skimming, skipping along, a mere 20 feet above land, following a lay line older than the Appalachians. I'm sliding down faster, and faster, and faster, until I've lost all feeling of movement, and now I'm here, right here where I have to be in order to move along, in order to finally rest. I have fallen from the sky into moonlit sand. I find my feet—I still have them, just energy, though, and somehow I can't quite stand straight. Okay, so I am slumped, and now I am falling sideways, and now a dog runs up, sniffing. She puts a bone in her mouth, rejects it. It's an old fish bone, not mine at all. Oh, I forgot, I don't have any bones.

I sit down, why bother to stand when I'm not of any substance? Even the seagulls can't see me, they fly right through me. I lie down on the soft cool sand, why bother to sit? I am looking up at the sky, a moon just one day past full, and if I stretch out my legs I can almost touch the vast green ocean with my skinny boneless toes. What else needs to happen? Can I go now?

White sand, easy surf, gentle wind, full moon.

My bones have turned into shards of sea shells—that's nice to see. My breath, the waves. My mind is an empty conch. I'm lighter than wind, lighter than the space between stars.

I am only watching the water, my thoughts done.

There is a sound of four-legged sandpaper footsteps, an animal being. My eyes are gone! I reach out to touch... my hands are gone! Suddenly, wham, I'm in a body, eleven years young. Runner has knocked me down. She's cleaner than snow and she smells like fresh rain. I am caressing her ears, and now she's running again, we're galloping down the beach together as fast as ever we ran during her days with me in the mountains.

That's it, poof!

Just a white light in the sand, a small eddy of foam, then another wave coming in, erasing everything.

A Patrilineal Genealogy

- Colleen Nicholson's twin brother Michael Bright Nicholson remained with the original family, 2 valleys over. Died 1965.

- Michael fathered one daughter, Michaela Nicholson Apple ("Ol' Granny Apple"), born 1902. Michaela became a mystic/healer & teacher of Lawrence Castleman. Died 2010. Her husband Clive Apple died 1931.

- George Bright Apple, a son, born to Clive and Michaela 1920. Died 1945.

○

Deep and enduring gratitude to Ken Lenington, Amy DeLap, and Susan Sluyter for their painstaking and patient editing assistance, delivered with unceasing encouragement and love I could feel.

Applause and laughter and thanks to my nanowrimo buddies Ingrid Jendrzejewski, Rachel Jendrzejewski, and Andy Jendrzejewski!

Huge love and appreciation to all who make life amazing (and worth writing about), especially our very dear ones
Sara Deter, Will Deter, Eric and Mary Lenington, Neal Wagner, Rahma Issa ….Pearl, Jensine, Jamal, Mom and Dad, Trish, Yvonne and Bob, Judy C., Paula, Ben, Andrew, Matt, Bekah ….Margaret and Josh, Bob F., Bob D., Linda D., Joan Lenington, Rob, Marissa, Dan, Karen, Naomi, Ella, Cameron, ….Ron, Marie, Shannon, Rachael, Brenda, Isaac, Jorge, Abbie, Kara, Madeline, Brent, Karen C., Diana, Elias ….Matthew and Daniel, Alayna, Roger, Mary Ann, Karen D., Susan G., Sue Brooks, Pam, Vivian, Doc & Annie, Nancy and Andrew, Harold and Ada, Lilly and Parsley,
oh my….. and oh my…

HA!

—Athie Wolfe

NOTES

www.ingramcontent.com/pod-product-compliance
Lightning Source LLC
Chambersburg PA
CBHW050743250626
47155CB00005B/1900